Erin stared in shock at the man she hadn't seen in one year and nine months.

Clay Griffin had changed. His face was leaner, his body harder. If anything, he looked even better now.

The lying, scum-sucking jerk.

"Get out. Please. We have nothing to say."

She tried to hide the trembling in her voice, but failed. Clay's face went hard as granite. He glanced at his watch. "We're out of time. You're going to have to trust—"

"Trust you?" She let out a sharp laugh. "Are you delusional? You left our bed one morning. You vanished. And when I called your so-called company, they said they'd never heard of you. You're a liar, Clay Griffin. If you said the sky was blue, I wouldn't believe you."

"I should've known I'd have to do this the hard way." He took a step toward her. She backed away. "You're coming with me."

"I'm not going anywhere."

ROBIN
PERINI

UNDERCOVER
TEXAS

H HARLEQUIN® INTRIGUE®

For Stephen and Jodi.
I'm blessed with a brother who possesses the heart of a hero
and a sister-in-law whose joyful spirit recognized the soul of
a burned marshmallow. Their devotion to each other and their
children is never-ending and awe-inspiring. This one's for you!
I love you both. Always.

ISBN-13: 978-0-373-69697-0

UNDERCOVER TEXAS

Copyright © 2013 by Robin L. Perini

Recycling programs
for this product may
not exist in your area.

Printed in U.S.A.

www.Harlequin.com

ABOUT THE AUTHOR

Award-winning author Robin Perini's love of heart-stopping suspense and poignant romance, coupled with her adoration of high-tech weaponry and covert ops, encouraged her secret inner commando to take on the challenge of writing romantic suspense novels. Her mission's motto: "When danger and romance collide, no heart is safe."

Devoted to giving her readers fast-paced, high-stakes adventures with a love story sure to melt their hearts, Robin won the prestigious Romance Writers of America Golden Heart Award in 2011. By day she works for an advanced technology corporation, and in her spare time you might find her giving one of her many nationally acclaimed writing workshops or training in competitive small-bore rifle silhouette shooting. Robin loves to interact with readers. You can catch her on her website, www.robinperini.com, and on several major social-networking sites, or write to her at P.O. Box 50472, Albuquerque, NM 87181-0472.

Books by Robin Perini

CAST OF CHARACTERS

Erin Jamison, PhD—The brilliant engineering prodigy fell in love with a liar. Now the man she gave her heart to has kidnapped her and their son—supposedly to save their lives. Can she trust a man who won't even tell her his real name?

Hunter Graham, aka Clay Griffin—A black ops warrior who lives in the shadows, Hunter Graham is on the most important mission of his life—to save the woman he can't forget and the child he has never met. Can he find a way to protect the family he always wanted but can never have?

Brandon Jamison—Hunter's one-year-old son can't know that his very existence has placed his parents' lives in peril.

"Doc" Fabiano—Hunter believed Doc was one of the good guys. He saved Hunter's life more than once, but did he also lead the terrorists straight to their safe house?

General Kent Miller—His elite team has no name and no designation, and Hunter is one of Miller's best operatives. Will the general be forced to sacrifice more than he ever imagined?

Terence Mahew—If the money's right, this former Special Forces soldier won't turn down the job—no matter how distasteful. But even he has to wonder if this time he's in over his head.

Leona Yates—Hunter's most trusted ally, she taught him the subtleties of clandestine operations. She's the only person who knows about Erin and their son. Has she sold out Hunter's family for a Swiss bank account?

Trace Padgett—General Miller's right-hand man has his own secrets. He can kill with one stroke, but where do his loyalties lie?

Chapter One

"We need a dead body."

"Yeah, Jimmy, we do, except we need two bodies for this job." From the passenger seat of their van, Terence Mahew scanned the suburban development they'd staked out. A lick of sweat trickled down his forehead. Blasted Florida heat. The van was hotter than some of the hell-holes he'd visited courtesy of the U.S. military before he'd been drummed out.

Terence swiped his brow with a bandanna, tied the rag around his shaved head and looked over at his eager-eyed cohort. "You wanna pick the vics this time? We need a woman and a kid."

His nephew nodded, face flushed with excitement.

Yeah, Jimmy was psycho. Just the way Terence liked his accomplices. Ready for anything. No conscience in sight.

Terence propped his combat boot on the dash, slid his favorite Bowie from the leather sheath on his thigh and tested the blade. The sharp steel nicked his index finger, and a drop of blood pooled on the pad. Bored with wait-ing, he considered the crimson bead for a few seconds, then smeared it across his skin. Interesting how the cut oozed and then stopped so quickly. He inhaled deep and sucked the salty fluid. Sick, he knew, but he loved that coppery tang.

Since being booted out of Special Ops, Terence had missed the kill. He'd put the word out to the right people, and he'd landed a sweet gig this time. A woman and a baby. Easy pickings.

The way he looked at it, he'd been lucky. Paid to kill since he turned eighteen. Of course, now the highest bidder wrote the checks instead of the government. His next paycheck had enough zeros to take care of his mama for quite a while.

Terence flicked his thumb against the blade, drawing another dollop of blood. He'd regretted the fear in his mama's eyes when he'd given her the new car his last visit. She never asked him a question or said a word. Just gave him that look, that same skittish, knowing look as when he was a kid telling her he planned to hone his "hunting" skills in the woods near home. Well, he was all grown up and still hunting. He expected she knew it. At least his prey was a lot more fun now.

Speaking of prey, Terence had a kidnapping to plan. He scanned the upscale neighborhood's surroundings beneath a hooded gaze. His nephew might be raring to go, but too much enthusiasm made a man stupid. Jimmy boy didn't need any help in that department.

His nephew needed to be cold and calculating, no emotions. That's what made Terence the best.

"Okay, Jimmy, tell me what you see. Anything useful?"

"There are some nice houses," Jimmy ventured nervously. "Lots of trees. Grass."

"Are you *trying* to piss me off?" Even with the air conditioner blowing full force in his face, perspiration soaked the back of Terence's T-shirt. Ninety percent humidity and ninety degrees pretty much sucked as much as the kid's powers of observation.

"Listen up, you idiot. We've been following Dr. Jamison

around for the past few days. Each afternoon we've been planted right in this spot, watching her. What does she do?"

"Uh…snags her kid from the car seat and cuddles him?"

"That's the hearts and roses version. We're kidnapping her. You need to identify what she does that will let us grab her and the baby. She pulls her car in right beside those great big bushes, takes the kid out and puts him on her hip, Jimmy. That means she balances all her other crap on the other arm so she has no way to defend herself."

"Do we kill the kid?"

"No." Terence had wanted to eliminate the baby, too. Easier to set up the disappearance that way. "The guy who hired us almost blew an artery when I suggested it. Apparently, his group needs Dr. Jamison alive and unhurt. They want her baby for leverage."

"Too bad."

"Yeah." Truth was, as long as the check cleared, Terence didn't care what they'd planned for the doctor or her kid. None of his business. But he'd bet she wouldn't be living in a small, peaceful suburban neighborhood with tidy green lawns anymore. From the rumors he'd heard about this terrorist group, she'd likely be held in one of the piss-poor desert countries he'd spent the past fifteen years crawling all over. The only way her kid would stay alive was if she did exactly as she was told. Terence could almost pity her, except he was too busy counting those tantalizing zeros.

He leaned his head on the seat rest and closed his eyes, envisioning the approach route to grab his quarry. Inside the house or out? Dusk? Full dark? What would be the best escape path? He wished he didn't feel like he'd missed something important.

He looked over at Jimmy. "You're sure she lives alone? No lover who's out of town or on a military assignment? She's got a kid out of wedlock, so she's no saint."

"I'll check again." Jimmy tapped his smartphone and chomped his gum, his fingers flying over the keys.

The kid's computer hacking skills were useful. Only part of his brain that worked right, but he could find out anything about anyone.

"No husband. No lover. No baby daddy coming round. No siblings. No parents. No one will care when she disappears…except maybe the geeks at the university where she works."

"She got a gas line going into the house?"

He flipped through a couple of screens. "Yep. Stove. Perfect setup."

"If the fire is hot enough, it ought to destroy the DNA."

Jimmy drummed his fingers on the steering wheel. "Can I pick the people we're gonna kill now? Please."

"Okay. I guess you've earned it." Terence scratched his chest. "Remember, we need a woman *and* a child." He turned his head and met Jimmy's glassy-eyed gaze. His nephew was already imagining the kill in his mind, just as Terence used to. "So, where do we hunt?"

"Ummm…the mall?" His nephew bit his lip and sent Terence a cautious glance.

"The mall." What an idiot. "Why don't you pick the damn police station? The mall means video cameras, and the victim will likely be someone with money and ties to the community. That'll trigger a missing person's investigation. Television, newspapers." Terence glared, gripping his Bowie knife tighter. "I'm not gonna get caught 'cause you're stupid."

Jimmy swallowed so loud the gulp echoed through the van.

Yeah, the kid should be scared. The moment he screwed up, he'd disappear. Nephew or not. "Try again. This time use your brain."

Jimmy bit his lip, his brow furrowing in concentration. "A homeless shelter?"

"Not bad." Terence nodded at his nephew's hopeful expression, then slipped the knife back into its sheath. "I like it. Take us to the next county. I know just the place." He'd stayed there when he'd first been discharged. No one wanted to hire a vet with his record. He'd been at rock bottom then.

He leaned back in the van seat, satisfied how things had worked out. The ones who had looked down on him were all six feet under now. He'd made sure of that.

Just like he'd make sure that Dr. Erin Jamison and her son would disappear tonight. The whole world would believe they were dead.

Terence laughed. Before those bastards were through with her, she'd probably wish she was.

HUNTER GRAHAM PACED HIS LIVING room, cursing the sweltering New Orleans summers that made him feel so trapped. He'd been edgy all day, with nothing to account for it. Except maybe thinking about a trip he wanted to take, but couldn't.

He stared out the huge glass front windows. Heat rose in shimmering waves from the sidewalk and the early afternoon sun flooded his living room with glaring light and oppressive heat. What idiot came up with the brilliant notion of lining three-quarters of the room with huge panes of glass in a state frequented by severe wind gusts, killer storms and hurricanes?

Deserts, horses and horned toads sounded better and better every stifling day he spent here. He'd have been long gone back to Texas if not for Erin Jamison and the baby.

Was she the source of his edginess?

He continued pacing like a caged animal. Erin was his

weakness. He had no friends outside the company. No family. No social life. He hadn't allowed himself a bit of softness since he'd screwed up and let Erin into his heart that week. What a stupid mistake seducing her had been. She and the baby could pay for that with their lives if his enemies found out.

Cursing one last time, he walked back to the state-of-the-art gym he'd set up in his living room.

Hunter centered himself on the vinyl seat of the weight bench, shoved the barbell straight up and locked his elbows. He focused on the weight, the tension in his arms, and pushed his feet into the floor, his entire body straining. Sweat pooled on his forehead.

Slowly, he lowered the two-hundred-fifty-pound bar to his chest. Aware of each muscle, he inhaled, then pressed up with a loud exhale. His arms trembled as he slowly lowered the bar back onto its stand.

God, he hated his existence. He wanted out. He wanted a life.

He wanted Erin…and his son.

Hunter's teeth ground together and he shoved the bar up again. He had to quit wishing for things he couldn't have. It was Logan Carmichael's fault. Six months ago, Hunter had spent his so-called vacation helping the ex-CIA agent stop a royal coup and some vicious terrorists who were trying to kill Logan and his newfound family. Carmichael was now the prince—and de facto security head—of the tiny European country of Bellevaux, ruling beside his wife, an ex-Texas cowgirl turned queen.

Seeing Logan so happy with his wife, son and daughter made unfamiliar envy rip through Hunter's gut. He'd given up his right to a family when he joined General Miller's clandestine group.

A loud tone buzzed on the wall screen. Someone at the

company making contact. Hunter let out another curse. He was on vacation, supposedly incommunicado from everyone and everything. He needed this time to pull himself together. Giving up on a dream didn't come easy.

Scowling, Hunter tapped the remote in his pocket. Motorized shades slid down the windows, closing out the sun. The room went dark momentarily; automatic lights came on and a large wall screen flickered to life.

Hunter snagged a towel, mopped his face and looked at the screen. Leona, his handler at the company. The woman who held his life in her hands. She'd let her hair go gray, and it looked good on her, swept away from her face. She wasn't a day over sixty, feisty as hell and an inveterate flirt. He adored her, and owed her for saving his life several times over, including on that last mind-shattering assignment. He didn't know how she'd pulled it off, but no one would have come home without her intervention.

"Hi, handsome, you are quite a sight," Leona's husky voice drawled over the video conference. "If I weren't married and old enough to be your mother, I'd eat you for breakfast."

He tugged the towel around his neck and smiled. "If you weren't married to the man of your dreams, sweetie, I'd sweep you off to an uncharted island and we'd live happily ever after."

"If the idea of me leaving my hubby behind bothers you, we can always invite him along."

Hunter laughed. "Whoa, Leona. You're too wild for me. I don't think I can keep up."

She sighed. "Yeah, that's the story of my life…."

Hunter shot her a grin, then turned serious. "So, I know you didn't call to make Chuck jealous. What does General Miller want? He agreed to my three-week leave and—"

"Vacation's been canceled. He wants you in Kazakhstan ASAP. Another high-risk op with limited intel."

Hunter fought the cold sweat that enveloped him. His last mission for the clandestine agency had gone to hell. Limited. Right. An intelligence screwup more likely.

All Hunter knew was that when the ambush came, he hadn't reacted fast enough. He'd been injured in the firestorm, but two members of the team had taken enough shrapnel to start a scrap metal business. Both men survived, but they'd never be the same. One would never walk again.

Hunter blamed himself. Those were his men, and his instincts usually warned him of danger. He hadn't seen this one coming.

"I can't go yet. I need some time." He'd felt driven to check on Erin and his son for days. Every fiber in his being urged him to take that trip to Pensacola. Maybe instead of torturing himself by watching from afar, he should say goodbye for good.

"Look, Hunter, Miller's not the only reason I'm calling."

Hunter tensed. Leona's voice had changed, taking on a note of urgency he recognized and that never boded well. He slipped on his sweatshirt to fight his sudden chill. "What's going on?"

A shadow crossed her face. Leona stiffened suddenly, peered over her shoulder and quickly looked back at her computer. In a businesslike voice, she said, "Yes, sir, I can get that information for you."

Confused, Hunter left the weight machines and walked over to the video system. "Are you talking to me?"

Leona shook her head slightly and tapped a few keys. "I'll forward the data to your desk."

When her visitor left, she rose and shut her door. "This has to be fast. Are you alone?"

Hunter caught the strain in her voice and, for the first time, noticed the worry lines on her forehead and bracketing her tight smile. "You have my attention."

Leona leaned forward in her chair. "Remember the *personal favor* you requested of me about a year ago?"

Oh, hell, no. *Erin.* Leona had heard something.

He'd prayed this day would never come. "Yeah, I remember." Hunter's stomach clenched. "Are we secure?"

"No one listens in on my encryption. Not even the good guys." Leona tapped her keyboard, and half the screen filled with translated transmissions. "As you can see, there's been chatter about Dr. Jamison for the past few weeks."

"Weeks? Why are you just telling me now?"

"It took a while for me to identify who the references specifically meant. Besides—" Leona quirked an eyebrow "—when did you want me to tell you? When your cover was getting blown by a rogue informant or during your latest firefight?"

Hunter shoved his hand through his hair. "Point taken."

"Besides, the intel wasn't specific enough until now. Hunter, she's in trouble."

"The info is verified?"

"Affirmative, and action is imminent. According to the chatter, one of the Seattle cells is making a delivery of human cargo tonight. *Your* cargo. Both of them. Final destination—unknown."

Hunter swore. "Get me off the Kazakhstan mission. Tell General Miller I've got the flu. I died. I've lost it. Whatever will work."

"Convincing him of anything is not easy these days, Hunter. You're his go-to guy for the tougher ops, and he knows you don't break. He said—and I quote—'I want him back in the saddle fast after the last trip's…*unfortunate* outcome.'"

Hunter stilled. "*Unfortunate outcome?* Half the team got shot up. Drummond and O'Reilly are still in ICU at the hospital, hooked up to a million wires and life support. Yeah, that's *unfortunate*."

Anger laced every word, but guilt lay heavy on Hunter's shoulders. There was plenty of blame to go around. In hindsight, he should have seen the ambush coming. Then again, the company should have, too, and well in advance. Either someone screwed up big-time or someone was out to get them.

"I *can't* go to Kazakhstan. Not until I know Erin is safe."

"I finagled what I could. You have five days before you have to report. I've already set the contingency plan you worked out for Dr. Jamison in motion."

"You're an angel." Hunter snagged his ready bag from the closet.

"The plane is fueled and standing by. You'll be at Eglin in one hour."

"Thanks."

"I've got your back…Clay Griffin. Don't mess up."

Clay Griffin.

An alias he hadn't used in almost two years. One he hadn't expected to hear or use ever again. Erin knew him by that name.

As Clay Griffin, he'd loved her, lied to her and left her, but it was Hunter Graham who dreamed of her every night, wishing he'd never been forced to abandon her and the child they'd conceived.

The moment he'd learned she was pregnant, he'd longed to go to her, but he had to stay away…to protect her and his son.

His efforts hadn't mattered, though. Erin's genius had put her in danger. Now he had to go to her, save her and his son, and leave them. Again.

Yeah, no doubt about it. His life pretty much sucked.

TERENCE TENSED AS JIMMY pulled the van into a run-down urban area and parked. They hadn't needed to drive far to reach the perfect hunting ground for people who wouldn't be missed. This was the land of the hopeless.

The surrounding streets were narrow and riddled with trash. Decrepit buildings loomed overhead, and seedy bars, with blaring music and falling-down-drunk patrons, fronted every other building. The homeless shelter huddled between an abandoned church and a boarded-up Laundromat. The haven of choice for the abandoned and invisible.

People shuffled in and out of the doorway of the shelter, heads bowed, defeated—and, to Terence's mind, disposable.

He rolled down the window. The stench of hot urine on pavement filtered into the van. He coughed, hating the filthy place, but encouraged that, from this vantage point, he could survey potential targets.

A few women with babies walked by. One was the wrong race. Another too fat. Still others were too short or too tall.

Normally, he enjoyed the selection process, but with time short, their lack of success made him nuts.

"What about her?" Jimmy said. "She's a match for Dr. Jamison."

Terence looked, then growled at his nephew. "The kid in the stroller is wearing a *pink* hat. Are you blind?"

Jimmy cringed in his seat.

Terence glanced at his watch, his frown deepening.

"We're running out of time. This is taking longer than I thought."

"There she is," Jimmy whispered, pointing to a woman at the far end of the block.

Terence raised his binoculars to check her out, not feeling particularly hopeful.

Right height. Right weight.

He sat up, his heart quickening as he took in the tattered blue blanket covering a kid just the right size. The kid must be sweltering, but he wouldn't suffer for long.

The combination was perfect.

Jimmy fairly vibrated in his chair. "It's them, right? What do we do now?"

"Start the van. Drive toward them, slow and easy," Terence crooned, his voice calm as he tried to quell his building anticipation. "We don't want to spook her. She took too long to find."

Jimmy turned the key, and the van's engine rumbled to life.

Terence squeezed between the seats and edged to the back doors. Snagging a wire from the toolbox with one hand, he placed his other hand on the lever. He loved this part. The surprise on the victim's face. The fear. Then, finally, the realization that death was imminent.

He couldn't wait.

"Not until she crosses the street," Terence warned.

Jimmy slowed the van to a crawl, and the vehicle eased alongside the woman.

Terence eyed her struggling with the stroller, one wheel wobbling when the blanket tangled around it. The woman shook her head in frustration, lifted the boy with one arm and tugged at the blanket jammed in the wheel.

"Now!" Terence called.

Jimmy slammed on the brakes; the back end of the van stopped beside the woman.

In one motion, Terence shoved open the metal panel door and hopped out of the vehicle. The woman's eyes widened. She opened her mouth to scream, but Terence clamped his hand across her lips, wrapped his other arm around her and dragged the woman and baby into the vehicle.

He flipped her on her back and straddled her legs. With one quick loop, he circled the wire around her neck and pulled, cutting off her air supply.

The baby rolled on the floor and wailed in desperation.

"Jimmy, grab the stupid kid and move out."

"It's screaming. Are you sure we need it?"

The woman's eyes bugged. She clawed at the wire, frantic to survive for her child. She kicked out against Terence and he laughed. She couldn't hurt him. He had her.

The van started moving.

"You gonna be quiet?" he whispered to the terrified woman. "Or do I kill your kid now?"

Immediately, the woman stopped kicking, her breath coming in ragged gasps. A tear trailed down her cheek, but she didn't move. She thought she could save her kid.

The brat made good leverage.

Maybe Terence's clients were smarter than he thought.

"Not a word," Terence warned her. He eased the wire off her throat, noting how the steel had left a red mark, but little else. He smiled. He knew exactly how much pressure would incapacitate, and how much would kill. He wrapped her wrists with the wire. "If you try to escape, this will burrow into your skin, slice through your tendons and eventually sever your hands from your arms. I don't suggest you try it."

The blood drained from her cheeks and she nodded.

He drew a finger down her cheek and lifted the tear from her face. He swiped the salty wetness with his tongue. Blood and tears. Ambrosia of the gods. Today was looking up.

"Please," she whispered. "Let my baby go."

He frowned at the Southern drawl in her voice, trying to place her accent. She wasn't a local. Maybe she'd never be missed. "I warned you to shut up."

He snagged some duct tape from the bin on his right and snapped it in place over her lips. He ran his fingertips down her arm and up again. The woman's skin erupted in goose bumps.

"You like that, do you?"

Quivering, she shook her head.

"Liar." He trailed his hand from her neck, over her breast to her waist, watching her cringe and flinch from his intimate touch.

"She'll do just fine, Jimmy." The woman's physique matched Dr. Erin Jamison's, down to the C-cup size. Terence glanced at his watch. "Our customers will be at the airstrip at seven tonight. We make the switch in four hours, deliver the goods and collect the money."

"What'll we do until then?" Jimmy asked, gripping the squalling kid in one arm as he struggled to drive without snagging the attention of the law.

Terence pulled a long strip of duct tape and shifted off the woman's hips, then moved down to bind her ankles. He slid his knife from its sheath and sliced through her shirt, leaving her stomach bare. One more swipe and he'd cut the frayed material of her cotton bra.

She whimpered as her full breasts spilled free.

He stared at the abundance of curves and smiled. "I'll think of something."

DR. ERIN JAMISON PULLED HER old Chevy into the driveway, shut off the car and fell back against the seat. The baby was sleeping in his car seat, and she couldn't muster the energy to move. She'd left work early to pick Brandon up at day care, but traffic on I-10 had been a nightmare. They were late getting home.

She hated the daily commute, but she needed to be near enough to her research, yet she needed a safe neighborhood with good schools for Brandon to grow into. Granted, he was only one, but she always planned ahead. Always...

Her life consisted of lists, five-year plans, schedules.

Her daily planner was her closest friend.

She was the proverbial "good girl," and except for the weeklong passion fest she'd indulged in Santorini that had resulted in Brandon's birth, she'd always colored inside the lines. The lines had been kind of blurry since then, but she still tried.

"Mama!"

Brandon's excited voice broke into her reverie.

She glanced over her shoulder at the little dark-haired wonder grinning at her as if she hung the moon. Her heart filled. She'd never regret that vacation. She regretted falling so hard for a lying, cheating, sexy daredevil who swept her out of her sensible shoes, but regret her amazing son? Never. Even though he looked exactly like his father.

"Ready for dinner, cutie?"

"Mama," he chortled. "Mama...mama...mama."

She smiled and gathered her purse, briefcase and Brandon's diaper bag, giving thanks that he'd finally moved past "Dada." It made her sad to hear that word knowing Brandon would probably grow up without a father.

It would be a heck of a long time before she trusted her instincts regarding the male population again.

She opened the car door with a sigh. What an energy-depleting day. She'd fielded dozens of calls from the organizers of the upcoming symposium in Switzerland, concerning everything from computer equipment to what kind of bottled water she wanted. Seriously?

Erin rounded the front of the car and opened Brandon's door. "Hi, cutie. Guess what?" She leaned in closer and dropped a kiss on his head. "Mommy's boss says that I'm a 'rock star' in nanotechnology. How about that?"

Brandon blew her a raspberry, then tugged a hank of her hair half out of her head.

Erin laughed, even as she rescued her locks. "Thanks. I hope the crowd at the symposium is more impressed by my status than you are."

After years of dedicated work through the nanotechnology department at Florida Tech, she headed a small research division in a little known location near Eglin Air Force Base. Erin's latest project had generated incredible buzz in the medical field. With her new working prototype, she could taste personal success on the horizon. Once she delivered the paper on her exciting breakthroughs in nanorobotics, she could write her own ticket.

She unclicked the top buckle on Brandon's car seat.

Clay Griffin, Brandon's disappearing Dad, had warned her off the project. Said she might attract the wrong kind of attention. Thank God she hadn't listened to him.

The leaves on the oak trees lining the street rippled in the slight breeze.

Despite the heat, a weird chill ran over her, as if she were being watched.

Strange. She glanced around quickly, but because of her intense work schedule she didn't know any of her neighbors. She recognized one or two cars by sight, maybe, but that was it.

After another few clicks to disengage the safety harness, she removed Brandon from his car seat. She balanced him on one hip and settled the diaper bag, her purse and the briefcase holding her laptop on the opposite shoulder. Suddenly, getting her son into the house seemed vital.

Brandon rubbed his eyes and nestled into her neck. She'd love nothing more than to spend the evening cuddling him, but she had a lot to do this weekend to prepare for the lecture. She'd officially present the prototype of her miniature robot at the worldwide conference next week.

The symposium organizers had kept the title of her nanorobotics presentation under wraps as long as they could, but her topic had started leaking out over the past couple of weeks. She'd been fielding questions from the robotics, engineering and medical communities ever since. Would the tiny robot survive the body's immune system responses? Would the technology work? So far, all the tests had exceeded her wildest hopes.

She walked toward the front door, Brandon tugging on her blouse. He threw her off balance, and the strap of her laptop slipped down her shoulder a bit. Her son had the same unsettling effect as his father.

"Oh, for heaven's sake, forget Clay Griffin," she complained. But how could she, when every time she pushed back the lick of hair from Brandon's forehead, she saw a miniature of Clay's face? Brandon's black hair and dark brown eyes were so unlike her green irises and blond locks. Clay's eyes had mesmerized her. She'd thought them a window to his soul.

"Yeah, and that foolishness worked out really well for you."

Once at the door, she fumbled for her keys and jostled Brandon. He giggled, squirming.

"You are such a wiggle worm." She stumbled through

the door, laughing. "Give me a minute and I can put you down."

A shadow crossed the floor in front of her. Her entire body went taut. She turned to run.

"Erin, wait! It's Clay Griffin."

It couldn't be...

"Clay?" She slowly faced him, staring in shock at the man she hadn't seen in nearly two years. He'd changed. His face was leaner, his body harder. His eyes a lot colder. The black T-shirt tucked into his black jeans outlined his sculpted muscles. He'd been breathtaking when she'd first seen him on the Santorini beach. If anything, he looked even better now...the lying, scum-sucking jerk.

"Get out of my house," she snapped, her voice dark with anger. She stepped aside and nodded at the open door. "Go. There's nothing for you here."

Clay didn't budge. "There's an emergency. We need to talk."

"No."

He took one step toward her and she backed up. His powerful presence filled the room, sucking the oxygen from her lungs. The man she remembered, the one still haunting her dreams, had been sexy. He'd intoxicated her senses. Facing him now, in reality, made her shiver. He looked dangerous. Menacing. Anything but the warm, romantic lover who'd seduced her.

Brandon wriggled in her arms, trying to get a look at the stranger. Clay's gaze fell on the boy and softened, became almost vulnerable.

"How'd you get in?"

"Your security is a joke. Shut the door."

A frisson of fear rippled up her spine. "And be alone with you? That worked out really well for me last time."

Clay shut the door himself. "You're in danger and we have to leave. Get your things together."

Sudden fear raced through her. "I'm not going anywhere with you."

Clay's face went hard as granite. He glanced at his watch. "We're out of time. You're going to have to trust me—"

"Trust you?" She let out a sharp laugh. "Are you delusional? You left me alone in your bungalow. No note, no phone call. You vanished. I called the desk and they said not to worry. You'd paid both our bills before leaving. That made me feel great, Clay. Tell me. Was it good for you, too?"

"Erin, we don't have—"

She cut him off, determined to get her say. "Yeah, we do. When I contacted your so-called company, they said they'd never heard of you. You're a liar, Clay Griffin. If you said the sky was blue, I wouldn't believe you."

He cursed under his breath. "Fine, we'll do this the hard way." He crossed toward her. "You're coming with me. You're the target of a kidnapping plot by suspected terrorists."

"Right." She grabbed her cell phone from her pocket. "I'm calling the police."

Clay pulled out a small electronic gadget and pointed it at her phone.

She glanced at the touch screen. *No signal.* No way. She recognized the jammer from a classified briefing she'd attended. Top-secret technology. "Who are you?"

He snagged her phone and tossed it aside, then grabbed her arm. "Erin, the men who want you are dangerous. Come with me now or you and Brandon could die."

"You're craz—"

A loud crash sounded at the back of her house followed by a dull thud in the kitchen.

Clay yanked his pistol free and shoved Erin behind him.

Two armed men wearing ski masks burst into the living room.

Clay raised his gun. "Freeze!"

The smaller of the two, barely more than a kid, skidded to a halt, his eyes widening with surprise. "Terence, what do we do?"

"Shut up and fire!" The taller man raised his own gun.

Erin gripped the baby, trying to stifle his panicked cries. Clay flew across the room and slammed one foot into the teenager's groin. While the kid writhed on the floor, moaning, Clay shifted, lightning fast, and kicked the gunman's arm, making his shot go wild.

The man named Terence cursed, but held on to his weapon, then faced off against Clay. "You've had training, pretty boy, but I'm still going to tear you apart."

Clay's eyes went dark and deadly. "Drop your weapon."

The kid staggered to his feet, blocking the shot, and Terence shoved the guy into Clay and fired.

Clay spun to the side, shaking off the kid, then dove at Terence's weapon. They grappled for his gun and it went off again.

The shot slammed into the wood near Erin's head.

She screamed and ducked down, holding her son tight. Her briefcase and diaper bag slid to the floor. Dragging them, Erin scooted backward toward the door. She had to get Brandon out of here. They needed help. Maybe someone had heard the shots and had already called the police.

Blood spattered the floor where she had just been sitting. She flinched as Clay slammed his fist into Terence's face for what was obviously not the first time. Blood spewed from man's mouth and he growled like a feral animal, his eyes wild and insane.

He gripped Clay's shirt in bloody hands and yanked Clay forward into a brutal head butt. Clay's head snapped back. He grunted, then twisted his body, grasped the madman's arms and flipped the guy over onto his back. The floorboards shook from the impact. Clay tried to pin Terence, but he kept fighting.

The younger man, dazed and wobbly, rose to his knees and started scrounging for his loose gun on the floor.

"Clay," Erin shouted. "Watch out!"

Unable to break away from Terence, Clay kicked the other man's gun away, "Get my backup weapon from my ankle holster and cover him."

Still holding the screaming baby, Erin scrambled to her feet, dashed over to Clay and yanked a small pistol from its holster.

The distraction gave Terence the advantage. "Fool, she's your weakness. It's every man for himself." He slammed his fist into Clay's kidney. He doubled up, and the thug pinned him to the floor. A second later, Clay retaliated, breaking the hold.

Erin caught movement from the corner of her eye and whipped the gun toward the smaller assailant. "Don't move," she warned him, flipping off the safety. "I'll shoot."

The young man looked at her shaking hands and sneered. "You don't have the guts."

He aimed the gun at Clay and Erin squeezed the trigger. A vase just left of the guy's head shattered. The kid dropped his gun, "Holy hell—" He thrust his hands into the air.

"Get down," she shouted. Brandon, hysterical now, screamed nonstop. She tugged him close, even as her finger twitched on the trigger.

Clay finally pinned Terence and jammed a forearm against the idiot's windpipe. "Who sent you?"

A small ding sounded on the guy's watch. He smiled. "Don't matter. You should've killed me and run. The house is rigged to explode in forty-five seconds."

Clay punched Terence and shoved him aside, then swept up Erin, the baby and her laptop and yanked them to the doorway. "Go! Go! Go!"

Still cradling Brandon, Erin stumbled through the door and took off across the lawn, her purse smacking off her legs. Clay was behind her, urging her to head left, toward her neighbor's property. Once they rounded the low hedge, she glanced back.

The smaller masked gunman staggered out, holding his crotch and breaking into a panicked run.

Terence followed, blood coursing down his battered face. "You're dead!" He bolted across the lawn, his gun raised.

Clay dragged Erin behind a huge Hummer in her neighbor's driveway and yanked the backseat door open. "Get in!"

She ducked her head as he shoved her inside, then crawled over her into the driver's seat. Bullets ricocheted off the vehicle and windshield. The Hummer had bullet-proof glass? She hunkered down against the floorboards, clutching the terrified baby, when a huge explosion rocked the car. Bricks, boards and flaming debris rained down on the lawn and the vehicle.

Dear God, her house had erupted in a fireball, flames licking the darkening sky like crazy, writhing snakes. The two men attacking them had been slammed to the ground. The psycho, his sleeve on fire, stumbled to his feet and raised his weapon again.

She bent down, sheltering Brandon.

Clay rammed the Hummer into gear and careened into the street. The car skidded and swerved, throwing Erin back against the bottom of the backseat. Her laptop and the contents of her purse scattered. She hugged her son to her chest, struggling for balance.

Clay gunned the engine and the Hummer lurched forward, speeding away in a squeal of tires. He careened around several corners, driving like a NASCAR racer until he finally slowed a bit. "You okay?"

"Not even close." Erin shook uncontrollably as the adrenaline drop racked her system. "Clay...who were those men? Why were they trying to kidnap me?"

He glanced back over his shoulder. "I'm pretty sure they're hired by terrorists."

"What? Why?"

"You *really* should've listened to me in Santorini. Why'd you go and finish that prototype?"

Chapter Two

"Terrorists want my nanorobots? They're medical devices. Not weapons."

"They can be adapted for military purposes."

Hunter ignored Erin's gasp as he considered the next phase of his plan. He'd hoped Erin would be a bit more amenable to coming with him, but he shouldn't have been surprised. In Santorini, she'd shown she had plenty of fiery passion hidden behind that cool scientist facade.

He studied the fire in the rearview mirror. The raging conflagration and plumes of thick black smoke had centered above the kitchen area. Natural gas explosion, no doubt. The neighbors were lucky the whole block hadn't gone up.

The gas leak would probably be labeled an accident.

Not a bad plan by Terence and his lackey. They weren't complete idiots. Arrogant, perhaps, and vicious, but apparently not stupid. One of them had major computer skills, based on the hits Leona had discovered on Erin's bank transactions. His handler had been impressed when she'd traced the activity and it had led to a dead end. Impressed, but not happy.

Hunter was counting on the computer guy to be good enough to tap into Erin's credit card usage to track her movement. The guy's skill could mean that the risky plan Hunter and Leona had devised might succeed.

"Did you hear me?" Erin snapped. "I need to be able to protect my son, and I can't without full disclosure."

Brandon was his son, too. "I'm kind of busy right now. We'll talk when we're safer." Hunter ripped the Hummer around a sharp corner, then maneuvered down little-used roads, driving evasively for a few more miles. Once they were clear, he pulled the Hummer over. He glanced at the pair bundled on the floorboard. He'd almost lost them. Five minutes later and Terence would have had them on their way to the handoff.

Hunter longed to tuck Erin and Brandon in his arms and protect them from the world, but he couldn't afford to let his guard down, even for a minute. Terence was right. Erin was Hunter's weakness, and his world hadn't changed. If anything, it had become more dangerous, and her nanorobotic prototype made everything worse.

"Those men were killers. We need to go to the police, Clay."

Hunter sighed. He was still Clay to her. A fictional computer security consultant who had vacationed on Santorini, made love to her and was essentially harmless—except to her heart. And now her life. She didn't know anything about him. Didn't know he sometimes killed people for a living.

"The police can't help," he said. "These people are out of their league. You're stuck with me."

"Great. I didn't realize you were a superhero. What if something happens to you? I go to the police then? Even though I don't know anything?"

Whoa, she knew how to skewer him on target. If he died, she and Brandon would be captive or dead. Hunter ignored the twist in his gut. Despite what he wished for in his stupid dreams, he had to keep his emotions in check. Erin's and Brandon's survival depended on his experience in high-risk operations. He couldn't let them down.

"I said that we'll talk. You can get up now."

Erin crawled onto the leather backseat, a worn-out Brandon in her arms. Hunter couldn't keep his gaze away from the sleepy baby as she rocked him, whispering words of comfort. The baby burrowed against the curve of her breast and settled in. He stuck his thumb in his mouth, closed his eyes and nodded off.

Hunter shifted his attention back to the road. "Will he be okay?"

"My son will be fine. I'll take care of him." She glared at Hunter. "I've been doing it on my own for quite a while."

"I guess we're going to skip the thank-you-for-saving-my-life part of this conversation, huh, Erin?"

She shot him a look. "Clay, I'm grateful. I'd be stupid if I wasn't, but I wish I was sure what you were *really* doing at my house. You have a car seat. Did you get it because you intended to rescue us, or did you plan to take Brandon the entire time?"

Hunter's throat closed off. He'd wanted to do just that so many times, but he wanted more than Brandon. He wanted them both. Hunter shook off the regrets. He couldn't afford to think of what could have been. "Instead of griping at me, why don't you put Brandon in the car seat and strap him in? You can trust me."

"My house is ashes. My son is in danger." Erin flashed an irritated look at Hunter in the rearview mirror but did as he said. "Excuse me for having trouble finding my happy place. Trusting you is just not happening, no matter what you've done for us."

He caught the tearful quaver in her voice hovering just below the anger. She was exhausted...and petrified.

She should be.

Way more than she realized.

"I promise...you'll be fine," he said rashly, having no clue if he could guarantee such a claim.

"I've been fine since you disappeared," she said. "Then, the moment I see you again, my home goes up in flames. You fight like an assassin and your phone-jamming toy is too high tech and top secret for a computer analyst, or whatever you're claiming to be today. If you're into something bad, how do I know you didn't bring this trouble down on me?"

He shook his head. Despite her fragile—and frightened—appearance, Erin Jamison had a spine of steel and a genius IQ that made her way too smart for her own good. Any other time, her suspicions about him would be correct, but this crisis she'd brought on herself. "I told you, your prototype caught the attention of the wrong people. My company intercepted several communications that indicated you were to be kidnapped tonight and turned over to a terrorist cell. Those are the facts."

Erin let out a shaky breath. "If you know who these people are, then drop me by the police station and tell them before you go. After they're arrested, I'll deal with this problem just like I've dealt with everything since I was eighteen. By myself."

For a smart woman, she was being incredibly obtuse. She was in danger. He wanted to be there for her. He'd always wanted to be there for her. When he'd been unable to get her memory out of his head, he'd taken his first clandestine leave to go see her, thinking he'd surprise her.

Instead, she'd surprised him. She'd been seven months pregnant.

He'd never doubted her child was his. She'd been a virgin before Santorini. She had been so naive. An unbelievable prodigy, genius level, and the most innocent, loving person he'd ever known. She'd made him feel alive again.

Seeing her pregnant, and knowing that even by communicating with her he'd endanger her *and* the baby, Hunter had gone from elation to grief in a heartbeat. Every warning from that first briefing with General Miller pummeled through Hunter's brain. No family. No friends outside of the team. No weaknesses.

Erin was his vulnerability, his child an even larger one. They could be used against him. He couldn't risk putting her, their child or his team in danger. His heart hadn't shattered into a million shards when he made the toughest decision of his life. It had been sucked into a black hole, where no feelings escaped.

He'd had no choice then.

Or now.

Hunter turned on a road leading to highway 281.

Erin whipped her head toward Pensacola. "You're going the wrong way. The police station is back there."

He flipped on his turn signal and merged into traffic. "Erin, I'm the only one who can help. I've devised a plan." Hunter pressed a button on his earpiece. "We're en route."

"Did you pick up the packages?" Leona asked.

"Yes, but our *friends* were less than five minutes behind," Hunter growled. "Why didn't you know about them earlier?"

Leona let out a curse that belied her grandmotherly appearance. "Must be new deliverymen. I'll look into it." She paused. "By the way, the firemen found the charred remains of two similar packages inside the burning building. Police are assuming they belong to the occupants of the house. I suspect they were delivered to the address just prior to the blast."

Hunter's gut roiled. He'd heard a thud in the kitchen

just before Terence and his partner had burst into the living room. He didn't want Erin to ever know what had happened. "Our friends don't want anyone searching for a missing doctor and her son."

He could picture the flash of fury in Leona's eyes.

"How do you want me to proceed?" she asked.

Hunter watched Erin's eyes. He could see those genius-level brain cells taking in his end of the conversation with his handler. Erin would understand the whole situation soon enough. As far as the world knew, she and Brandon were dead. Hunter didn't intend to change that perception.

"Stay with the plan, Leona. Run the credit card as soon as we've had time to get to the marina. Track any hits so I know when they're coming our way."

"Done."

The scratch of pen to pad filtered through the phone. Leona was nothing if not old-fashioned. The brand-new tablet computer the general had issued her lay unused in her drawer. Paper was more secure, she'd told Hunter defiantly when he asked about the unopened box last time he'd visited headquarters.

"We still on the down-low?" he asked.

"For now. Not sure how much longer I can keep a lid on it, though. I'm getting looks."

"Be careful, Leona."

"Don't worry." She chuckled. "I'll have my husband call and talk dirty to me. That should back them off from listening in on my conversations."

Hunter quirked a smile. "Poor Chuck."

"Don't pity him. He'll get thanked very well tonight."

"TMI, darling…. Keep in touch." He tapped his earpiece and glanced back at Erin once more.

Her jaw ticked with barely restrained frustration. "Who are you, Clay? You're way more than a consultant."

"Someone who wants you to stay alive. Let's leave it at that."

"I deserve the truth," she said finally.

He couldn't argue there.

Brandon fussed and squirmed for a minute. A pungent odor wafted through the car.

Erin wrinkled her nose. "I think we have a dirty diaper, and his bag never made it out of the house." She looked down at an increasingly unhappy Brandon. "He needs changing. Can you find me a store?"

Hunter had spent two years on the streets and in shelters. He'd watched over enough helpless kids when their mothers were too strung out to change a dirty diaper. He knew what kids needed. Diapers, food and toys. He'd expected to pack Brandon and Erin's things at her place. Did they dare stop?

"It's got to be quick," he muttered, even as he checked ahead for a place to turn off.

He looked at his watch and tapped the earpiece to hail Leona.

"Miss me so soon?" Her lilting voice was tinged with worry that most listening would miss.

"We're making a stop. We'll use the card here. Monitor our location and adjust the timeline for when the information goes out."

"Roger that."

Hunter swerved into a superstore parking lot and turned in his seat. "We don't have any leeway in our schedule."

The flare of anger and trepidation in her eyes was quickly doused, replaced with determination.

He didn't like that look. He scanned the parking lot before exiting the Hummer's door and opened the back. "Let's go."

She got out, then lifted Brandon. "You don't have to come with us. I can run in and out while you keep watch."

Her gaze flicked left, a tell for lying, and it pissed Hunter off. "I can see right through you, Erin. You are *not* bolting with *my* son."

She gasped. "What makes you think Brandon's yours? You're not the only man I've slept with."

The words sliced off a piece of Hunter's heart, and doubt raced into his mind for a split second. Then he realized her eyes had flicked again and recognized the ploy. General Miller was right. Family made you soft.

"Don't lie to me again, Erin. First off, you suck at it, and second, it's unworthy of you."

She twisted away from him. "But it's okay for you to lie to me?"

"To save your life? Absolutely."

Erin tensed with anger, and Brandon whimpered and squirmed against her hold.

"Besides," Hunter said, fighting the trembling in his hand as he touched his son's soft black hair. "I knew the second I saw him he was mine. He's a miracle I never expected to exist."

Erin's eyes filled with tears and she looked away.

Brandon stared at his father as Hunter brushed his hand down the baby's chubby cheek. The boy laughed and grabbed Hunter's finger, squeezing tightly.

Hunter grinned. "Hey, sport, you're pretty strong for a little guy."

Erin gulped, but she didn't pull away. "What do you want from us, Clay?"

He met her gaze. "What I can't have," he said, knowing it was the first truly honest statement he'd made that night.

"Let us go," she whispered.

"I can't."

Her grip on Brandon increased, and he let out a squeaking cry.

"The baby needs changing," she said. "We'll talk again later."

"I can't wait," he muttered under his breath. They hurried across the parking lot and entered the store.

Within seconds, Hunter identified all of the exits, then cataloged each potential hiding place and every person within his line of sight. No one appeared interested in them, and his equipment didn't indicate any tracking devices. They were relatively safe for the moment.

Erin grabbed a shopping cart, settled Brandon on her hip and made a beeline to the baby section. Hunter pressed his arm across her. "I go first. *Everywhere.*"

Now-familiar irritation crossed her face. "Lead on. I just thought we were in a hurry."

What had happened to the shy, gentle woman who'd let him take the lead in the bedroom? Then again, when he'd asked about her work, she'd blossomed into a confident, brilliant woman he hardly recognized. He'd loved the dichotomy. He could kiss her with passion and leave her trembling with want, but when he'd warned against finishing the prototype, she'd turned into she-devil.

Hunter finished his scan of the surrounding aisles and nodded to Erin to go ahead. She gave him another aggravated look and headed for the diapers.

As she searched through the plethora of colors and sizes, he admitted that he'd been awestruck by Erin's idea, but he also recognized the inherent danger if the device was misused. He clearly hadn't made a strong enough argument to stop her.

"You almost done here?"

She didn't respond. From the corner of his eye, he saw

her pause and stare at two swinging doors at the back of the store.

He bent close. The floral scent of her hair wafted near him and he breathed in deeply. His lips moved against her ear. "Don't even think about it," he said, his words soft and firm.

She bit her lip. The disappointment in her face would've been funny if he wasn't fighting for their lives.

He took a breath. "I'll make you a bargain. Let's deal with Brandon's problem. Then I'll take you somewhere safe. After you've heard the details, make your decision."

"If I don't like what you have to say, you'll let us go?" she challenged.

"Yes," he lied. She could never go back to the life she'd known. Not anytime soon. And once her identity changed, he'd never be able to see her...or his son...again.

He ignored the shriveling of his heart at the thought and glanced at his watch. "We're running out of time. Too many cameras around here that could be tapped into."

Startled eyes met his. "These people are that sophisticated?"

"You'd be surprised."

She frowned. "Okay, I've had enough security briefings to know it's possible. I won't take a chance with Brandon." She grabbed a diaper bag, baby powder, wipes, clothes, a small blue train, a ball and a couple of jars of unappetizing-looking mashed-up food.

Poor kid.

"Get whatever he needs for a while," Hunter said softly. "In case you stay with me."

She narrowed her gaze, then nodded, but she was obviously troubled as she collected several more of everything. "I'm ready."

"What about you?"

She huffed, then quickly pushed the cart to the women's section. She tugged jeans and T-shirts off the sales rack, but bypassed the lingerie.

He lifted an eyebrow.

She blushed, grabbed a few serviceable cotton bras and pairs of underwear, and tucked them beneath the other clothes.

He had to smile. She had nothing to be embarrassed about. Her breasts were larger since having the baby, and she'd been impressive before. He'd explored every inch of her body. What he'd give to peel those slips of cotton off her and reenact a time when they'd been safe and warm.

To distract his thoughts, he snagged tennis shoes and socks. "Size seven?"

She nodded and he dumped them into the cart.

He wished he could talk honestly to her, tell her what her future really held. It was too soon. Instead, he simply led her to the checkout center. "Use your credit card." He handed her a large stack of twenties. "This should reimburse you."

Erin gaped at the wad of cash and pulled out her debit card.

"No." He grabbed her wallet. "This one." He took out the American Express and handed it to the curious clerk.

It was way past Brandon's naptime, and the baby sobbed in Erin's arms. Nothing would calm him. She snagged a juice box from the bag and placed it in his hand.

"No!" His cries went full force, and big tears rolled down his face.

"Fis…" He lurched forward, stretching out his entire body as he reached for the goldfish-shaped crackers moving past him. Unbalanced, Erin lost her firm grip on him.

Before Brandon landed on the conveyor belt, Hunter

scooped him up with one arm. "Sorry, sport. You're not on sale today."

The clerk giggled and it hit Hunter that he was holding his son for the first time. Granted the kid stank, but it didn't matter. He cradled the boy carefully, and Hunter's heart melted. He'd never imagined the impact one tiny being could have. He devastated Hunter's defenses.

"Give him to me."

He didn't want to give Brandon back. "Sign the credit slip first."

As Erin wrote her signature, Hunter couldn't take his gaze away from Brandon's every feature. The baby's nose was like Erin's, but his mouth was like Hunter's mother's.

Odd. Hunter hadn't thought of his mother in ages. He'd pushed aside his memories of his less-than-stellar childhood years ago, and yet she was here in the face of his son.

He held up a finger, and Brandon grinned and grabbed it, trying to stuff Hunter's large knuckle in his mouth.

Erin held out her arms. "He's mine."

Her words sent a flash flood of cold water across Hunter's emotions. Erin was right. He couldn't let himself get attached. Yet, as he placed Brandon in Erin's arms, Hunter knew he'd already made that mistake.

He'd fallen in love with his child. First through the photos and often-grainy surveillance videos he'd managed to procure over the past year, and now that Hunter had held his son...

God, he was a fool.

With a heavy sigh, Hunter led Erin to the exit and paused. After a few moments of scanning the exterior, he nodded for Erin to move. They quickly crossed the parking lot. Once they reached the black Hummer, Hunter opened the back end and pulled out the duffel bag he'd planned to use during the operation.

After her reaction to his lifestyle already, he doubted she'd appreciate the weapons and equipment inside. He hadn't had time to get passports with new names for her and Brandon. She'd have freaked for sure, seeing those.

He and Leona had designed dozens of more dangerous missions than this, but never had more been at stake. He hadn't planned his overwhelming reaction to Erin—or his son.

While Erin changed Brandon's diaper, he whined and reached for the cheddar-flavored crackers again. She disinfected her hands and gave him a few. "He's hungry. It's dinnertime."

"What can he eat?"

"He's teething. I bought some soft baby food I can feed him in the car. His favorite is mac and cheese, though. He loves it."

"So do I," Hunter said.

Erin sent him a sidelong glance. "I didn't know that."

"My mom would make it as a special treat when she was working." He made room for the diapers in the duffel. "I haven't thought of that in a long time."

With efficient movements, Erin had Brandon settled in his car seat, then handed him a soft ball that he stuffed into his mouth and gnawed on happily.

"You're quick," Hunter said.

"Practice."

Something he'd never have. Hunter closed down his emotions. In moments, he'd packed the remaining items, including Erin's laptop, in the duffel and closed it carefully, making sure the fastenings created an airtight, waterproof seal.

He scanned the parking lot again. "We've got to go now. That credit card swipe started a stopwatch."

Hunter slipped into the front seat and tapped his earpiece to contact Leona. "We're done. We're heading to the marina. Start the electronic bread crumbs. Once our *friends* ping the credit card and find us, I want all transactions to disappear. We can't leave the cops a trail that they can easily follow."

"Got it," Leona said. "How long a lead time do you need?"

Erin got in beside him and buckled up.

A minute later, he pulled out of the parking lot. "The traffic's heavy. Give me at least fifteen minutes. They need to see everything for this to work."

Leona sighed. "Are you certain you want to do this?"

Hunter looked at Erin and Brandon. "I have no choice," he said quietly and ended the connection.

Erin and Brandon Jamison had to die. Today.

ERIN FIDGETED IN THE FRONT seat, battling urges to jump out of the car or give Clay the trust he asked for. Brandon was in the backseat, so she knew she was staying put for now. Clay *seemed* to care about Brandon, and she couldn't deny those men had broken into her house, shot the place up and torched it. She'd almost been hit by more than one bullet.

"This is crazy," she muttered. "I can't believe I'm letting you take us to the Gulf of Mexico. I barely know you and what I do know scares the pants off me."

"Excuse me while I savor that image," Clay said. "I'm saving your life. You know I'm right."

"I don't know anything anymore." Her temper frayed, her emotions in turmoil, she hated that somewhere in the deepest recesses of her mind she'd dreamed of Clay coming back to her, pulling her into his arms. He'd convince her that he hadn't lied, that she hadn't been wrong about falling in love with him, that they could be together.

What a stupid fantasy.

As stupid and unreal as her sitting beside him right now with no idea where they were really headed.

She'd graduated from high school at sixteen, college at nineteen and received her doctorate in nanotechnology at twenty-three. She was no dummy, so why was she just sitting here, letting the miles go by? She couldn't take her gaze away from Clay's strong, tanned hands gripping the steering wheel. Focused and determined, he constantly swept their surroundings with the awareness of a wild animal ready to pounce on its prey. She could barely recognize in him the man she'd fallen in love with on Santorini.

Then he'd been gentle, funny, romantic. Everything she'd ever wanted.

Had she been completely wrong about him?

Could a man change so completely? Or be so completely deceptive? Had she ever known him, or had she only seen what she wanted to see?

Or what *he'd* wanted her to see?

She shifted in her seat. "Were you *ever* in computer security, Clay?"

His knuckles went white. "In a way. I'm pretty handy with zeroes and ones."

"That means no. Who do you work for?"

"I can't say."

Her pulse pounded in her temple.. "I have a top-secret security clearance."

"Not high enough."

Erin nearly growled at him. "I've had enough of the cloak-and-dagger stuff. How do I know you didn't blow up my house? That this hasn't been some elaborate setup?"

Clay twisted in his seat. "Do you really think I would put my son in danger?"

"I don't know, do I? Because I don't know you. Where are you taking us? And why won't you tell me anything?"

"You'll understand soon."

"Not good enough." She snatched his phone and hit 9-1-1. He leaned toward her, but she unsnapped her seat belt and catapulted into the backseat.

"Erin…"

"No. I've given you all the chances you're going to get."

"Do you need a pickup?" a woman's concerned voice filtered through the phone.

Something was terribly wrong. "You're supposed to say *'Nine-one-one.* What's your emergency?' Who is this?"

"Code!" the woman demanded.

"I ne…need help," Erin stuttered. "I've been kidnapped."

"Dr. Jamison?" The woman's voice lowered. "Where's… Clay?"

"Noooo." Erin dropped the phone to the floor.

Clay pressed his earpiece. "Sorry, sweetheart. Didn't mean to give you heart failure. Things aren't going quite as *smoothly* as I'd like here."

Clay met Erin's gaze in the rearview mirror, and she glared. "You can't hijack 9-1-1. It's illegal."

Brandon whimpered, but Clay ignored them both, obviously focusing on the woman's voice on his headset. Someone he clearly cared for.

"Sorry, Leona, I'll try not to let my equipment get out of my reach again."

He disconnected and sent Erin an uncertain look.

"Please. Just let us go," she whispered. "I won't tell anyone about you. You can go do your covert ops stuff somewhere else, and no one has to know you were here."

Clay didn't respond at first. He maneuvered the vehicle onto a bridge over the water. Redfish Cove sparkled as the sun moved lower in the sky. Several kayakers paddled toward shore.

"Let me get you to safety first. I'll show you the evidence. Then we'll talk."

"I can't tell if you're lying."

His brown eyes darkened. "I know. I'm good at it."

"That's not something to be proud of."

His lips tightened. "Probably not."

Tense silence between them bathed the interior of the vehicle. A loud laugh erupted from the baby. Erin glanced at Brandon's joyous glint when he triumphantly pulled out the blue train, but she couldn't smile. Her world had spun out of control.

"Is Brandon okay?" Clay's voice had grown even more tense.

"He's fine," she answered woodenly. "He found his train."

Brandon jabbered as he rolled his hand against the wheels. A popping noise erupted from the toy, and he giggled.

She moved closer to her son. The moment Clay stopped the car, she had to escape. She had friends at Eglin Air Force Base. Surely someone there could help her.

Clay crossed a second bridge and finally pulled his Hummer into an out-of-the-way marina not too far from Pensacola Beach. He parked near a slip and tapped his phone.

"We're here. I'll be in touch when it's clear."

He opened the door and moved to the back, grabbing the duffel. Erin exited the vehicle and rounded the car to retrieve Brandon. She held him tight, glancing around, hoping to get someone's attention.

But no one was around. The marina had obviously seen better business days. An old man struggled into a dinghy down the way. She saw a couple of Jet Skis and a few rinky-dink boats tied up at the dilapidated dock. Other than that, the place was deserted.

She had to buy time. "Where are we going?"

Hunter headed to the water and snapped the cover off a cigar boat, its sleek lines putting to shame the other crafts. "Somewhere we won't be found."

"I'm not taking my son onto the water when it'll be dark soon. Are you crazy?"

"More than likely."

Erin clutched his arm. "I'm not going with you, Clay. I can't do this!"

"You don't have a choice." After grabbing her around the waist, he lifted her and Brandon into the boat. She fell back onto the seat, fuming.

Hunter flipped a midsized life jacket to her. "Put it on."

She shoved the orange flotation device aside. "You hurt me."

He leaned over her, trapping her between his arms. "Erin, if I'd wanted to hurt you, I'd have let you stay at your house. Now get your jacket on."

His movements quick and efficient, he bundled a squalling Brandon into his life jacket and settled his son on his hip. "Feel free to leave, but Brandon's coming with me."

"You have no right—"

"So sue me," he snapped. "That is, if you live through the next attack by your kidnappers. They're almost here, so move it, sweetheart, or none of us will make it."

Hunter settled in the pilot's seat behind the steering wheel.

With a curse, she followed, slipped on the life jacket and took her place in the copilot's position. She had no choice. She'd never leave without Brandon, and Clay's comments about the kidnappers terrified her. Her bravado was an act, with Clay receiving the brunt of her fear.

Hunter handed her the baby, then tapped his earpiece. "We're in place, Leona. Are they here?" He paused. "Okay."

The engine roared to life, the sound hurting her ears. She clutched Brandon close, rocking her terrified son, trying to shield him from the noise.

Hunter pressed the throttle forward. The floor vibrated beneath her feet as he eased the boat away from the dock, then picked up speed.

"Where are we going?" she yelled to Clay.

"A safe house," he shouted back.

Loud curses sounded from the shore. She whipped her head around. Two ski-masked men jumped on two nearby Jet Skis. One larger, one smaller. Her stomach dropped.

"They're here!" She turned to Clay, frantic. "How did they follow us?"

Erin froze at the cold look on his face.

"I left a trail for them. I wanted them to find us."

Shock slammed through her system. "You did this on purpose? Oh, my God…."

Clay jammed the boat into higher gear, and the craft skittered across the top of the water. Erin's heart raced. The men behind them followed, their Jet Skis jumping the waves and gaining on the boat.

Clay maneuvered around an inlet and into the Gulf of Mexico. He skimmed along the beaches, weaving to and fro, but he didn't lose the men following.

"They're still with us," she shouted. "They're getting closer."

"I know." He eased off the throttle and when he reached a straightaway of water, Clay attached a strap to the wheel to hold it on course. He reached out his hand. "Do you trust me?"

"No."

"That's okay. I'll save your life anyway."

Their attackers maneuvered alongside their boat and raised their weapons. "Give us the doc and the kid!" Terence yelled. "We'll let you live."

Clay ignored them. He shoved Erin and Brandon to the deck, crouched down and snapped off a small door on the side of the boat. Just large enough for them to fit through.

"When I open this panel, you slide out into the water and push away from the boat. The duffel floats. Use it to support you."

He kicked out the fiberglass. Seawater washed over them.

Erin's heart raced. "What about Brandon? How will I—"

"I'll bring him."

Panic hit, but she before she could protest, a bullet struck just to the right of Clay's head. He ducked. Another spray of bullets strafed the boat, coming way too close.

"Go!" he yelled. "Now!"

Swim or be shot? She had to trust Clay. She took a deep breath, looked at her son, then launched herself out to sea.

Water rushed over her. She sputtered and whirled around. The cigar boat sped away, and the duffel floated toward her, riding the boat's wake. She swam to the bag and wrapped her arms through a strap on the side. Frantically, she searched the water for Clay and Brandon.

Where were they?

Suddenly, an explosion shot fire into the sky.

The cigar boat burst into flames, the conflagration engulfing the Jet Skis and the men riding them. Oily smoke billowed across the waves.

"No!" The roar of the fire drowned out her scream.

Erin swam frantically toward the burning wreckage, but no one could have survived that explosion.

She stopped, finally, treading water, tears pouring down her face.

What could she do? They were gone.

Clay and Brandon were gone.

Chapter Three

The concussive force of the blast hit hard. Fiery debris, smoking upholstery, broken glass and sharp pieces of hot metal shrapnel rained down on Hunter as he curved his body around his son's to protect him.

Blazing chunks seared his neck and shoulders. The life jacket protected his back from the worst of it, but not all. He dipped lower in the water, hoping to extinguish the smoldering embers and ease any burns. After a few seconds, the thunderstorm of debris ceased.

A stark, stinging pain still stabbed under Hunter's shoulder blade, but he concentrated on survival, pumping his legs beneath the water. He'd kept the baby alive—hysterical, but alive. Now to find Erin. Waves rose and fell around them as he sought her out. Where the hell was she?

Brandon coughed and cried some more, and Hunter intensified the treading motion to lift the baby higher in the water.

Suddenly, Hunter caught sight of a still, mostly submerged figure facedown in the water. Blond hair floated on the surface.

Erin! A vise tightened around his chest. Hunter secured his grip on the baby and swam closer, cursing and praying he was wrong.

The surf tossed the body, turning it so Hunter had a better view. It was the kid, the smaller of their two assailants. Half the young man's body was shredded from the explosion, the jeans and shirt floating in bloody, tattered strips.

Hunter exhaled in relief, even when he hoped there were no sharks around that had been drawn to the blood. He certainly was bleeding, and Erin might be, too.

He had to find her fast, and they had to get out of the sea.

Hunter wiped the salt water from his eyes and kept scanning frantically. Terence had vanished, and Hunter could only hope the psycho suffered the same fate as his buddy.

"Mama," Brandon cried out, sobbing, grabbing on to Hunter's life vest and trying to climb over his shoulder.

"Mama! Come." The baby's voice held a tinge of anticipation.

Hunter craned his neck, searching for the source of the boy's excitement. Sure enough, the sunset caught the blond of Erin's hair in the water. She was twisting and turning, searching for them.

"Erin," Hunter called out. "We're safe. Get the duffel."

The waves drowned out his words, so with Brandon still clutched against his chest, Hunter kicked toward her.

She finally looked his way. Her emerald-green eyes widened when she saw them. She leaned back, glancing at the sky as if sending up a prayer.

The surf fought against him. Slowly, he worked his way closer to her.

"Mama, Mama!" Brandon called out.

Hunter surged two more strokes to meet her. Even with the salt water bathing her face, he could make out the tears.

"I thought you'd both died." She hugged her son, and the baby clutched her neck. She checked every exposed inch of the baby, then looked at Hunter, fear and gratitude in her eyes.

"Thank you for saving him," she whispered, her voice thick with gratitude. "He's everything to me."

Uncomfortable with the depth of her emotion, Hunter glanced over his shoulder at the remains of their cigar boat. It was still burning, with only parts of its smoldering hull visible above the waterline.

Far in the distance, a Coast Guard boat propelled its way rapidly toward the debris.

Hunter gauged the distance to the wreckage, then the shore. He hoped they were far enough away that they wouldn't be seen.

"We have to get out of here," Hunter said, his throat raspy from the smoke. "We can't be discovered. Will Brandon grab hold around my neck?"

"Yes, but just for a minute. He's only one."

Hunter swore, trying to figure out how to swim, balance the baby and keep his head out of the water, as well.

"Wait. I have an idea." Erin grabbed two of the carabiner clips she'd used to attach her purse to the duffel. "I use these to hang my keys on my purse so Brandon doesn't walk away with them. I hook his toys on, too. They should secure his life preserver to yours."

"Smart idea."

She kissed the baby's cheek. "You're going for a ride." She placed Brandon on Hunter's shoulders and hooked their life vests together. She wrapped the baby's little arms around Hunter's neck. "Hold tight, sweetie."

Brandon panicked, grabbed on and squeezed.

"Man, the kid has sharp nails." Hunter shifted Brandon a little higher on his back and shoulders, ignoring the pain from the burns and cuts. One wound hurt the most, as though the metal was still embedded inside. Hopefully, the salt water would help keep the burns from blistering and clean the others.

The drone of the Coast Guard boat drew closer. Time was up. He pointed to an inlet about thirty degrees to the right. "Erin, paddle toward that beach. There's an airboat waiting for us."

They started swimming. "Pace yourself. It's farther than it looks. Turn the duffel the long way and float on it for the least resistance while you kick. It will help."

Hunter kept checking that his son's hands were still secure; then he picked up more speed. Brandon squirmed, nervous about the water and jostling motions, and thrashed his legs. One little foot hit Hunter's worst injury hard, and he grunted as pain seared into his back and across his rib cage. What the hell? Maybe the shrapnel was still in there.

Hunter sucked in a breath and pushed on. Nothing mattered as long as he got Erin and Brandon to safety.

Erin looked over at him, her breathing coming fast. "You okay?"

"Yeah," he said through gritted teeth. "Keep going."

He was having a little trouble lifting his arms out of the water. The inlet looked so far away. Using a modified breaststroke, he continued to make progress, Erin by his side. Thank God she was a strong swimmer.

He scanned the surroundings, seeing only the rise and fall of waves and the occasional osprey soaring over them, searching for prey. He paused and did a quick eggbeater kick to rise higher in the water. His legs didn't respond as usual, but he ignored it.

He took in the chaotic scene. The Coast Guard cutter hovered near the burning skeleton of their boat. He let out a sigh. So far so good. The lingering fire and the boat engine would hopefully cover Brandon's cries. Still, the

Coast Guard boat would start circling the area soon, looking for survivors.

He and Erin started off again. Stroke after stroke, he hauled his increasingly weary body through the water. The inlet came within reach.

Hunter's back throbbed, but he was strangely thankful. That one sharp pain actually helped him stay alert. He kicked his legs, hating the unfamiliar weakness. "We're in the tide," he yelled to Erin. "It will help pull us in."

Her face showed her fatigue as she nodded. He let the flow of the water carry him toward the west side. A few seconds later, the silhouette of the airboat, with its distinctive fan on the back, came into view.

"That's it," he shouted, pointing at their transportation.

Brandon whimpered and Hunter clutched his son's wet hands around his neck. "Almost there, buddy."

Poor kid hadn't had a nap or a break from life-threatening situations all day. He had to be exhausted.

By the time they finally reached the airboat, the pain in Hunter's back pulsed with agony. The baby had kicked and hit every wound Hunter had with amazing precision. Kid had a great future in torture and interrogation.

Hunter pulled alongside the boat and groaned as he loosened his son's hands from around his neck.

Erin nuzzled her son's cheek. "Mama's here, little guy."

She quickly released the carabiner hooking the baby to Hunter, then tugged the shivering little boy into her arms. "He's freezing."

"Give him to me, then climb on," Hunter ordered. "I'll hand him to you and you can warm him up."

She nodded, handing Brandon over, then looked up at the flat hull. She swung her leg onto the base of the airboat and, with a bit of struggle, dragged herself safely onto the platform. "I can take him now."

Hunter winced as he lifted Brandon up to her. Hunter felt as if he had a knife in his back every time he moved. His burns hurt more as the air hit them, too. Thank God neither Brandon nor Erin was injured.

Erin sank down just in front of the passengers' double seats and cuddled the baby, checking him over. Hunter shoved the duffel over the side onto the boat. He took a deep breath, placed his hands on the edge of the boat and heaved himself up.

His back spasmed, and he couldn't hold his weight. He let go and slipped back into the water. The water eased some of the pain.

"Clay?" Erin leaned forward. "Are you all right?"

He gritted his teeth. "I'm fine."

Bracing himself more, he hauled his aching body over the side and onto the deck. He lay facedown, panting, waiting for the shooting pains to stop.

The boat rocked a bit, then settled.

"Oh, my God," Erin gasped. "You're bleeding."

DUSK HAD FALLEN BY THE TIME the Coast Guard ship left the accident scene and headed down the shore. Salt water lapped against the dock, under which Terence hid, sliding in and out of consciousness. With each rising and falling wave, Terence groaned in agony. From the amount of blood in the water, he was amazed every shark for fifty miles hadn't tried to join him.

Jimmy hadn't made it. Terence's sister would be upset, but it couldn't be helped. The kid hadn't been strong enough or determined enough to survive. Getting his arm and leg blown off hadn't helped. He'd bled out in a matter of seconds. Predators had probably finished off the job the explosion had started.

Dizzy and in agony all over, Terence wondered if he

would survive. He couldn't see out of one eye, and his whole left side was bleeding and burned from the explosion. He couldn't feel the side of his face. He raised one blistered hand and touched his cheek, or what was left of it. Nausea and horror hit. He wasn't just temporarily blinded. His face was like hamburger, and his eye and part of his cheek and ear were gone. He puked into the water. This couldn't be happening to him....

Gagging, he grabbed the dock's post with his good arm and jerkily hauled himself along the side of the pier. Finally, he stumbled onto the sand and crawled. He scanned the surrounding beach and found it surprisingly deserted.

He tried to move the fingers on his left hand but couldn't. He couldn't even feel them.

His mind raced. He knew burns were bad. But burns you couldn't feel were deadly. He needed help fast. Taking a deep breath, he hauled himself onto the roadway leading away from the pier. He slipped, smacking his arm and face off the pavement. Pain seared through him and he screamed, the sound echoing across the water.

No one came to help him. No one heard. He wanted to lie there and die.

Sorry, Mama. I won't be helping you after all. He couldn't stop the tears running down one side of his face. He lay still and panted until his mind could work again. He didn't want to move but he had no choice. He couldn't be found here.

Taking a deep breath, he struggled to move the left side of his body. Finally, he shoved himself to a standing position, then staggered back to the van and squeezed the driver's door handle.

Locked.

He fell against the side of the van, smearing blood

across the white paint. He didn't have the keys. Jimmy had been driving. What the hell was he supposed to do now?

Unless...

He rounded the vehicle to the other side, and the passenger door opened. He hadn't locked his door. One of his bad habits finally paid off. He flicked the button to unlock all the doors and braced himself to move. He was getting weaker. All he wanted was to go unconscious. He stumbled to the driver's side, lay partway down on the floor beneath the dash and yanked out the ignition wires.

Blinking against the blood dripping down his face, Terence worked them until a spark ignited. The engine pulsed to life.

He shoved himself into the van and glanced at the mirror. A hideous creature stared back. A huge lump rose in his throat. He was a monster. Even his own mama wouldn't recognize him. The entire left side of his face was bathed in blood and crusty blackened skin. He couldn't see his eye, couldn't lift his eyelid. He wasn't even sure they were there anymore. He was bleeding to death. He needed a hospital.

He sucked in a deep breath and, using his good arm, placed the truck in gear and headed toward the nearest road. He'd seen a sign indicating a hospital nearby. Somewhere... Blood dripped down his face. His vision blurred in and out, and his body sagged as if weighted with cement.

He didn't have much time before he blacked out.

He drove erratically, weaving side to side, and squinting against the last beams of the setting sun. Street sign after street sign rose to meet him. A few he took out with the van as he momentarily passed out.

A hospital sign loomed, an arrow pointing to a large building half a block away.

Almost there. He could make it.

A shrill ring sounded in the van. It took a minute to register that it was his phone. He fished around until he found the cell phone he'd left behind on the seat, rather than risk losing it in the water.

He glanced at the screen. This call he would take.

"Mahew," he croaked in a harsh, raspy voice that sounded nothing like his own.

"You are late," the familiar voice with the smooth British tone and Middle Eastern accent snapped through the speakerphone.

Easy money? What easy money?

"You didn't provide all the information," Terence growled, trying to stay conscious enough to guide the van to the emergency room. "You didn't tell me about the freakin' ninja protecting the woman. I lost my partner, and I'm half-dead myself. Check the news. Their boat exploded in some marina and took out two Jet Skiers. That was us."

"Their boat exploded? The woman is dead?" A string of foreign curses spewed through the phone. "If she is dead, you are, too. I have friends who will make certain that your liver will be a sacrifice, and your family will receive your head to remember you."

"Chill out. She's not dead. It was a setup. Some guy with serious skills rigged the boat to blow. No bodies have been found, other than Jimmy's, but I saw some shapes in the water nearer to the shore. I couldn't tell, but I'd bet it was them."

"Graham," his contact muttered.

"You know the guy?" Anger gave Terence a small burst of energy. "If I live through this, he's mine."

His contact ignored the comments. "You must find them. My…customer…is unused to delay. He will *not* be pleased. The situation could turn ugly."

"I'll give you ugly. Half my damn body looks like I

went through a meat grinder," Terence said. "I couldn't incapacitate the baby right now."

Terence's vision grew blurry. He tried to steer the van toward the emergency entrance door. He blinked, then blinked again. The van slammed into a wall and shuddered to a stop. Thrown forward, Terence smashed off the steering wheel and hit the windshield.

Sirens went off, waking him. Terence heard someone yelling.

A medical person opened his door. "Get a stretcher. Now!"

"Where are you?" the tinny voice on his speakerphone shouted.

Terence feebly lifted the phone to his mouth. "Hospital…"

His head slumped, and Terence groaned as someone reached in to move him. They bumped his left side and he screamed.

"We need an O.R. stat. Tell the burn unit to stand by."

"What is going on? Who is that talking?" The accent grew thicker.

His client's shrill voice brought Terence out of his stupor again.

"My new best friends," Terence drawled. "By the way, I quit."

He let the phone drop to the floorboard and slumped forward into the arms of the waiting medics. This time, all those damn zeros on a check weren't worth it.

"CLAY!" THE AIRBOAT SHIFTED back and forth with the waves. Erin clutched Brandon in her arms and tried to edge closer to the man bleeding, facedown, on the deck. At her movement, the boat tilted.

"Da…owie! Mama, Da owie!" Brandon threw a fit at the sight of all the blood.

She paused to move the boy so he couldn't see, then eased her way over to Clay's still body. He hadn't said anything. She couldn't see a wound, but the parts of the shirt visible beneath his life jacket were soaked red. Balancing Brandon, she reached for the life vest. Her fingers fumbled at the fastenings.

Clay groaned and tried to move.

"Be careful. Some of these cuts are bad. We have to stop the bleeding."

"I'm fine." He rose to his hands and knees. "Just a little dizzy. We have to get out of here. We're not safe."

He stood and grabbed hold of the pilot's seat, steadying himself. "Sit down and hold the baby on your lap," he said, nodding at the double-wide passenger bench in front of the perched captain's seat.

Not knowing what else to do, Erin followed his instructions.

She watched him steer the boat. He didn't even flinch, though every movement had to be agony. His clenched jaw was his only giveaway.

Today had shown her a whole new side to Clay that scared her. He was so hard and…tough. The man she'd fallen in love with on Santorini had swept her off her feet, made her laugh, made her tremble for the touch of his lips.

He even let her drone on endlessly about her prototype, nanotechnology, engineering and every other geeky topic that flitted through her mind. Most men's eyes would have glazed over, especially when she'd gone off on the potential of her discovery for miniaturization.

Clay hadn't derided her. He'd listened. Really listened.

But now that she thought about it, he'd shared nothing about himself in return. How had she not seen that?

She didn't know what to do. She hated uncertainty, and Clay Griffin was an enigma.

Erin buckled Brandon onto the vinyl bench and secured herself before settling him against her. She kissed the top of his head.

Clay eased into his seat, flipped some switches, turned on the key and the huge fan behind the boat roared to life. Within seconds they were skimming across the water toward a swampy maze of tributaries.

"We're going in there?" she shouted over the noise.

"Yeah, it's not far," he yelled. "I need to concentrate."

She remained silent, studying the determined set of Clay's jaw, his focused vision.

Her son's resemblance to his father didn't stop at the black hair and brown eyes. She'd seen the same look of determination on Brandon's face as he struggled to stand on his own. She'd wondered where her son got his stubborn streak. Now she knew.

Erin was single-minded, but Brandon took willful to a whole new level.

Brandon stuffed his fist into his mouth. She rocked him back and forth.

The gears shifted and the boat pulsed forward. They had to be edging against the engine's limit of about forty miles an hour.

She gripped her son tighter to protect him from the wind. The sky had begun to darken fast; their visibility decreased by the minute. She squinted across the deepening blue of the water as the light began to fade.

"How much farther?" she shouted.

Clay didn't answer. She twisted in her seat and looked up at him.

His face had grown pale, and sweat beaded on his forehead. He moved the steering stick forward with his left hand, then swayed. The boat veered right; he corrected it.

She didn't see anything he'd had to avoid. "Clay. Are you okay?"

He didn't respond. She tapped his knee. "Clay?"

He looked down at her, almost as if he'd forgotten she was there. "What? Oh, right. Clay," he said, his words a little shaky and forced. "We're almost there."

"You don't look good." Panic tinged her voice. She tightened the belt around Brandon. She might have to climb back there and take over.

"Just a little light-headed. It's nothing." He blinked again, then stared around.

He let out a loud curse. "Hold on. There's our turnoff." He pushed the stick forward and accelerated hard. The boat veered to starboard. They whizzed into a narrow channel.

A moment later, he eased off the throttle and the boat slowed, maneuvering into an eerily serene tunnel. Mangrove trees hung over them like a canopy; the ferns and palms edged closer and closer. The unfamiliar scents were cloying.

The boat skimmed over the surface as the airboat pushed deeper and deeper into the channel. The snake-like waterway grew increasingly marshy. Erin glanced at her side. What she thought was a rock nearby moved; it raised the blunt snout. An alligator.

She gasped and clutched Brandon closer, watching the creature submerge again.

"Clay, are we going to die before we get to this supposed safe house?"

He didn't respond. He released the throttle, and the boat drifted toward the water's edge.

The outgrowth of plants and roots infiltrating the water made it appear almost solid, as if they could walk from side to side of the narrow passage. The boat shoved the jigsaw puzzle of green plants out of their path.

An image of stability, yet filled underneath with danger and predators.

Much like her life from the moment she'd walked into her door only a short time ago.

Clay slowed the boat until he reached a small dock. The hull knocked against the wooden planks with a dull thud.

Erin peered past a wall of cypress trees, then saw a ramshackle wooden house half-hidden by the foliage. "Please don't tell me we're staying *there?*"

Clay turned off the motor, his eyes closed, and he let out a long sigh. "It's better than it looks. There's solid steel plating between those walls and bulletproof glass in most of the windows.

"Most?"

"It's a work in progress. I didn't expect to need it this fast."

"Remind me to time my attempted kidnappings better next time." Erin unbuckled herself, then Brandon. He whimpered in her arms as she rose.

Clay's eyelids snapped open. "Is the baby all right?"

"Brandon's fine. You're not," Erin said. "You look like you're going to keel over."

Clay pushed to his feet. "I'm fine." He swayed slightly. "I've got to secure the boat."

"I can do it."

He shook his head. "You need to know how to tie an anchor bend."

She exhaled. "You mean the knot where you run the line twice around that ring, twice around an object and do two half hitches? *That* anchor bend?"

His mouth dropped. "Okay, then…"

"I have a photographic memory. Just sit there and I'll

take care of it," she said. "Are you all right to hold Brandon?"

"Yeah," He held the baby to his chest before sinking gratefully into the captain's seat.

Uncertain, she hopped out of the airboat and quickly tied off the craft. She checked out Clay. Even though his eyes were closed, his arms held Brandon securely. His skin looked gray and it wasn't just the dark. He clearly needed medical attention. Clay had to have a good eighty pounds on her. No way could she carry him.

She gently grabbed hold of her son. Clay tightened his arms.

"Clay, it's me."

Her voice seemed to soothe him. He loosened his hold. She stood on the small pier. She couldn't put Brandon down, short of placing him inside the shack.

"Can you get out of the boat?" she asked, studying his every movement. If he fell into the water, she'd never be able to save him.

"Of course." Clay shoved himself to his feet. His jaw tight, he clutched the back of the captain's seat, then stepped on the pier. "See, I'm fine."

"Yeah, you're ready for a marathon. I want to get a look at your back."

The shack appeared as if it might fall down any moment. Clay flicked the latch and pressed inside. It seemed like a regular hunting shack, until Clay flicked a switch on the wall. A wall slid open, revealing a stash of weapons, ammo, a first-aid kit and other supplies.

A regular-sized bed took up one corner.

"Lie down," she ordered Clay, her tone brooking no argument. "I need to look at your back."

He shook his head. "Not on the bed. Floor. You and Brandon need a place to sleep."

"Just shut up," Erin snapped. She grabbed a couple of trash bags to protect the bed and then covered them with a sheet.

"Move it. I need you conscious and healthy to get us out of here."

Clay didn't argue. He eased himself onto the bed. "Just give me a minute. I'm sure the burn will go away. I'll be fine."

SURF SOUNDED IN HUNTER'S EAR. Heat beamed onto his back. From the landing off his bungalow, he faced the ocean, the ebb and flow of the tide against the black sand calling to him. The clear blue of the Aegean Sea teased the shoreline, advancing and retreating.

He shifted his stance, the knife wound on his side pulling against the sutures. Someone had fouled up big-time. His cover had been blown. He'd spent a hellacious month in captivity and had barely gotten out of Iran with his head attached to his body.

General Miller had sent in a rescue force. His boss could have left him for dead. Maybe should have, but the general would never leave anyone behind. He was loyal to a fault.

Hunter just wished he'd had better news for Kent Miller. The first report after Hunter had regained consciousness had been the one to inform the general that his son, Matt, hadn't made it. He'd died in that hellhole, with the bastard terrorist laughing.

Hunter had tried to save Matt. He'd failed. Hunter still didn't know why he had survived.

General Miller hadn't blinked at the horrific news, hadn't missed a day. The next night the terrorist camp had been decimated by a smart bomb. One less group to murder.

Now all Hunter wanted to do was forget.

A figure in a one-piece swimsuit and a billowy wrap strolled along the beach alone. The sun kissed her blond hair. She crouched down and her fingertips traced in the sand. She picked up something—probably a shell.

She turned to her side. The full curves of her breasts and hips were perfection. She stilled; then as if she'd heard his wish, she faced him.

Her head tilted, and she simply stared.

Now that was a thing of beauty. A definite means to forget.

He strode down the beach toward her.

As he approached, she looked from side to side.

There was no one else on this private beach. They were alone.

His feet sank into the warm sand. And then he stood only a foot from her.

Her eyes widened. Beautiful, emerald-green irises framed with dark lashes.

He couldn't stop from staring. She was absolutely perfect, and he wanted her.

She shuffled uncomfortably under his gaze and looked away, but strangely, she didn't run, she didn't pull away. She simply stared up at him, eyes wide.

"Hello there," his voice said, low and steady, wanting nothing more than to hear the sound of her voice. "Shell collecting?"

At first she appeared confused. She looked around as if he'd made a mistake.

"Me?" she asked.

He couldn't stop the grin. "Yes, you."

She smiled and held out her hand. A flat shell with a distinctive star-shaped design lay in her palm. "*Spatangus purpureus*. This is a small one, only about six centimeters." Her smile was bright, and her lips kept moving, going on and on about larvae and its life cycle. He couldn't respond; he could only be tempted by the smoothness of her skin and listen to the lilt of her voice.

Suddenly, she stopped and toyed with her fingers. "Sorry. I get carried away. I'm sure you're not interested in marine biology." She bowed her head and started away.

"Don't apologize. Wicked smart is very, very sexy," he said softly, his words forcing her to pause and turn back with a strange hope lacing her eyes.

Her shyness hypnotized him. He took the small shell from her palm and stroked its markings. *"Porfyrí kardiá achinós,"* he said, feeling the need to show her wasn't an idiot, even if he only had a G.E.D.

Her lips parted in surprise. "What did you say?"

"It means purple heart sea urchin."

Her eyes lit up. "You speak Greek?"

"Languages are easy for me," he said. "I speak a few." Mostly those of the world's hot spots so he could blend in. Turkish, Arabic, Kurdish, Persian, with a bit of Russian thrown in for good measure.

He returned the shell to her.

She slipped it into the pocket of her swim wrap and bit her lower lip. "Well, it was nice—"

"You're from the States on vacation?" he interrupted. He didn't want to let her go.

She tucked her hair behind her ear. "Florida. This trip is more of a celebration, I guess. I just successfully defended my dissertation and decided to go somewhere I'd always dreamed of. After living in the library, I wanted to see something amazing and beautiful."

She looked out over the sparkling water of the bay. "Did you know some scholars think Santorini might be Plato's Atlantis? The Minoans were far ahead of their time compared to the rest of civilization...." Her voice trailed off. "Sorry, there I go again. History this time."

She folded in on herself. Hunter couldn't allow that. "Would you like to go to dinner?" he rushed out. "With me. I want to hear more about the Minoans."

She swallowed and met his gaze. "Who's asking?"

He held out his hand. "I'm Clay Griffin." For the first time in a long while, using an alias didn't feel right. Not with this woman.

She laid her small palm in his. "Erin Jamison."

"Well, *Dr.* Jamison, how would you like company in your celebration? I can promise great food, great wine and perhaps more, if you're so inclined?"

Her cheeks flushed, and her pupils dilated with a flash of desire. The sounds of the beach muffled, and all Hunter could hear was the sound of his heart thudding. All he could feel were the shivers of anticipation skirting over his skin.

She licked her lips. He swallowed. Blood pooled low in his belly. Despite her shyness, this woman's sensual nature begged for his touch.

With a gentle hand, he stroked her cheek. "You are one intriguing woman, Dr. Jamison. Meet back here? Tonight? Six o'clock?"

She twisted the fabric of her wrap and folded it across her body. "I'd like that, Clay." With a slight smile she turned and wandered down the beach, every few feet staring back at him.

My name is Hunter.

He wanted to shout the truth, but he couldn't. She could never know.

Hunter watched the sway of her hips as she disappeared behind an outcropping of volcanic rocks.

With a sigh, he returned to his bungalow. He shouldn't

go tonight. Her eyes were honest, guileless. He was a man of lies, and he'd made a career of them.

But he'd be right here fifteen minutes early tonight, just as surely as he'd known the moment he'd taken his oath as a member of the armed forces that he'd finally found a place to belong.

He sighed, rubbing the bandage on his side. He would heal. And he would return to the team that had become his family, and try to redeem the loss of Kent Miller's son.

The surf lapped at the black sand, then melted away.

The sea transformed into a small room.

Hands pushed at his side, rolling him one way, then another. Someone tugged at wet material sticking to him.

His back screamed in agony.

No. He wanted Erin. He didn't want to let her go. Not again.

He twisted away from cloying hands. Erin was gentle. She would never hurt him. He was the one who'd hurt her.

"Clay!" A hand shook him. "Clay, can you hear me?"

He hated that name. He wanted only one thing before he left Erin. He wanted to hear her whisper his *real* name before the dream faded away—as they always did.

"No. *My name is Hunter.* Not Clay."

Chapter Four

Stabs of pain peppered Hunter's neck and shoulders, dragging him out of the dream. Not a dream. A memory.

And one that was long gone and could never be again.

The mattress shifted.

Hunter rolled to his side and forced his eyes open. Erin stood only a few feet away from him, holding Brandon, disbelief and hurt painted on her face.

"You lied about your *name,* too?" The accusing voice made him wince. "Just who are you, Clay, aka *Hunter?*"

He froze. The fog around his mind lifted. She hadn't said, she couldn't have said—

Oh, man, she knew his name. What else had he revealed? He'd been trained never to disclose important information. He'd faced guns and knives, swords and fists, and he'd never whispered his true identity. To anyone.

He groaned. "Can you forget I said that?" he asked.

"Was anything you told me the truth? Not that you said much. Whenever I asked you a question…" Her voice trailed off and her cheeks flushed.

Hunter knew exactly what she was thinking. The moment was etched into his brain. He'd had more than one dream about it. She'd asked him about his job, and how often he'd traveled. He hadn't wanted to lie—an unfamiliar urge—so he'd done the next best thing. He'd kissed her.

The first time, her cheek. The second time, her lips. The third time…he'd started at the arch of her foot and worked his way up, not missing an inch of skin.

They hadn't talked again for a long, long time.

How could he answer her? Wasn't it better for her to hate him? Wouldn't it make the next steps that much easier for both of them?

"Sometimes the truth isn't an option."

He sat up and grimaced. Man, his back hurt.

Erin and the baby blocked his path. "Oh, no, you don't. I said I'd look at your back and I will. As much as I want to kill you, I don't want your death on my hands."

He had to know the extent of the injury. Every movement of his shoulder blade burned like fire. He needed her help, even if she'd prefer to leave him to rot. If his injury got her mind off his name… "There're some basic supplies in that first-aid kit," he said, his voice cautious. "Next to the weapons."

"Yeah, I'm not even bringing up the irony there."

Erin pulled out the medical kit and placed it next to him, then opened the small refrigerator. Okay, so she was mad. She had every right to be.

Within seconds, she'd settled Brandon on the floor by her feet. He held a sippy cup in his small hands and stared up at Hunter. His son's big brown eyes looked at him with such trust…so unlike his mother.

And why should she trust him?

He unfastened his life vest and let it fall to the floor.

"Oh, Hunter," Erin murmured.

He blinked. Blood stained the inside of the orange material. He tried to look over his shoulder. Pain sliced through him and he hissed.

He lifted his arms to unbutton his shirt. She pushed his hands away. "Let me."

Her voice had gentled. Her fingers worked their way down, but when she tried to slide the material down his back, he couldn't stop the moan.

She stopped. "I'm sorry."

"Just get it off," he bit through clenched teeth. "The wound needs to be cleaned."

Together they worked his arms out of the shirt, but the material stuck to him.

"You're going to have to soak it off."

Resigned, Hunter turned onto his stomach. Erin filled a bowl with water, then returned to his bedside.

"This is going to hurt, Cl—Hunter."

Great. So much for hoping she wouldn't remember. "I know it's going to hurt. Let's just get it over with. I don't want Brandon seeing it."

She hovered over him and sucked in a deep breath.

"Do what you have to do," he said.

Her hands more gentle than he deserved, she wet down the shirt. Inch by agonizing inch, she pulled the cotton from his body.

Her gasp echoed through the shack.

"Hunter, you've been shot."

THE SECRET FACILITY BASED JUST outside Langley, Virginia, defined *covert*. No one used names here. Leona Yates wiped her hands down her dark suit, nodded at the guards and proceeded to the hand scan. Several seconds of whirrs and clicks later, the computer had matched the palm print, and a retinal scan had completed authentication.

"Yates, Leona. Verified," the mechanized voice confirmed.

She crossed the lobby and pressed a single button. Within moments a solid titanium elevator whooshed her down several levels. With the security and background checks, this was one place Leona had always believed invulnerable.

Now she couldn't stop her belly from twisting as she grew closer and closer to the man she didn't want to face.

The doors slid open and Trace Padgett waited to greet her. His strong, powerful figure impressed her, as much for his brains as his well-proven abilities to get the job done. No matter what the obstacle. Which was why her boss had handpicked him.

"The general's waiting, ma'am," Trace said, and held out an arm to escort her into the inner sanctum.

She nodded and walked down the barren hallways. "What does he know?" she asked.

"More than we do, most likely," Trace said.

"He always does."

Leona licked her lips and entered the general's office. He cut an impressive figure, his Special Forces experience keeping his eyes sharp and his intuition keen. They were about the same age, but the general's forehead carried twice as many worry lines. More responsibility. More decisions. More deaths on his hands.

Leona just prayed three more wouldn't come about on their watch.

General Miller crossed his arms. "Status," he ordered.

"Terence Mahew was admitted to a Florida hospital. He's alive but vulnerable. We should bring him in."

The general nodded at Trace. "Make it happen."

"Yes, sir." Trace saluted and exited the room.

"You trust him?" Leona asked quietly, revealing for the first time her discomfort.

Her boss's eyebrow rose, and then his jaw set. "I have to."

"Kent—"

"Why didn't you come to me, Leona? I would have helped you."

She squirmed under the piercing gaze. "I made Hunter a promise. I couldn't break it."

"You may have cost him his life." Kent's jaw pulsed with barely controlled fury. "He's been compromised. And somehow we have to fix it."

He drummed his fingers over his forearm. Leona recognized the look. "You have a plan."

"Maybe. I need more intel before I commit. Interview Mahew. Find out who his contact is. We have to identify the leak, Leona. Hunter is too valuable an asset. I *won't* lose him."

"Or his family," Leona added.

Miller nodded. "I want to know everything Mahew knows—and what he doesn't realize he knows."

"And after?"

"He's murdered at least two innocent people. Do what you think is best."

With a swallow, Leona gave him a small nod and walked to the door leading from Kent's office to the situation room. She turned back to her longtime colleague. They'd known each other since their training days. "Kent, I don't like how this is going down. In fact, I don't like much of anything that's happened over the past month or so."

The general sank into his chair, for the first time showing a fatigue she'd never seen. They'd been through hell together. They'd lost too many men over the years. Was she getting too old for the business? Maybe after this thing with Hunter worked itself out, she'd retire with Chuck and move to the Bahamas. Sea, sand, surf, frosty beverages, no thinking and no terrorists chasing after the people she cared about.

"We'll fix this, Leona. We can plug the holes on this *Titanic.*"

"It may not stop the ship from sinking, Kent. You know that as well as I do." She walked through the door, and the lock snicked closed behind her.

A wall's worth of monitors greeted her with a flurry of activity. Videos played from all around the globe. She made her way over to a Florida map and the newest addition to the team. Zane Westin had come in on Hunter's recommendation. He stared at the screen and punched the keyboard in front of him. She'd find out soon enough how good he was. "What's Mahew's location?"

A small red dot blinked in front of her. "Burn unit."

"Any other information?"

"We've lost track of Graham. He landed at Eglin yesterday. An unidentified boat exploded off the Florida coast. It matches Hunter's M.O."

Leona didn't comment. She knew all of this. "What about the chatter? Any new indications popping up?"

Zane frowned. "I don't know why intel wasn't picking up the signs before. Seems obvious to me. A bigwig scientist, Erin Jamison, was mentioned weeks ago."

Zane rattled off Erin's impressive bio.

"Current status?"

The computer jockey's expression grew grim. "She hasn't been seen since leaving her office yesterday afternoon. Two bodies were recovered from her burned-up residence. The cops believe she and her one-year-old son died in an accidental gas explosion. It hasn't hit the news yet."

Leona stared at Zane. "What do you think?"

"I don't buy it," he said softly.

Leona nodded. Hunter had been right. This guy *was* intuitive and smart. Or he was a fantastic plant.

"Okay, Westin. Not bad. See if you can pinpoint the origin of the chatter." Leona leaned down, her lips near the man's ear. "And Westin" she whispered, "don't give the information to anyone but me. Understood?"

Zane's gaze met hers. "Yes, ma'am. I understand."

Leona straightened. "I hope you do."

ERIN PRESSED HER FINGERTIPS near the deepest wound on Clay's back. She'd seen enough movies and television to know a bullet hole when she saw it. The projectile had torn through his flesh.

This would have laid most people out. And yet he still functioned. His color had even improved.

He shifted and tried to roll over.

"Can't you follow orders? Just this once?" The humidity clawed at her like a wet wool blanket, oppressive and stifling, not to mention that the dampness was a perfect breeding ground for bacteria. She pressed her hands against his left side—the only area not injured. She had to keep him still. She wiped her forehead with her sleeve. "Or do you want to get infected?" she snapped.

She leaned over on Clay's arms, trying to keep him from turning over, and pressed her mouth against his ear. "If something happens to you, what are we supposed to do? At least let me clean the wounds."

Brandon jabbered, holding up his arms to her.

Clay glanced over his shoulder at their son. His gaze softened, and then he scowled at her. "Get it over with," he gritted. "And don't be gentle."

She chewed on her lip. She didn't want to make him hurt worse, but sometimes there had to be pain to heal.

She knew that firsthand.

Erin blinked several times. The weeping burns looked painful. The life jacket had protected him, but not everywhere.

Brandon tugged at her pant leg.

"Hey there, cutie. What can we do to distract you, hmm?"

She glanced around the room and strode to a rickety armoire in the corner.

Brandon whimpered, crawling after her with that odd movement kids used on hardwood floors. Even her one-year-old avoided pain with each motion.

With resolve, she ripped open the doors and riffled through the wardrobe's drawers. One held some T-shirts, sweatpants and a few socks. She tied a sock in a knot and knelt down to her son.

"Can you play with this for a while, big boy?"

He clutched the makeshift toy and stuffed it into his mouth, grinning up at her.

"Is he okay?" Hunter asked.

"He'll amuse himself."

"While you have fun torturing me?"

"I may be mad at you, but I don't want to hurt you."

"Sorry, lame attempt at a joke. You look so intense."

"Who wouldn't?" She picked up the bloody shirt and life jacket and tossed them into the sink, then filled a bowl with water. She took the iodine out of the first-aid kit and squeezed a few drops into her basin.

"What are you doing?"

"Sterilizing the water and trying to keep infection from setting in." She grabbed a thin rag. "Are you ready?"

"Did you lock the door?" he asked.

"Of course. That rickety fastening may not keep anyone out, but at least it'll keep Brandon inside."

A loud bang sounded. She whirled around, then shook her head. Her son had discovered a pot and had turned it into a drum. *Bang. Bang. Bang.* He chuckled.

Erin sighed. At least he had distracted himself. Ignoring the incessant noise, she carried the supplies back to the bed.

"He's enthusiastic," Hunter said.

"You have no idea. I need the energy of two, and even then I doubt I'd keep up." She took in a deep breath and stared down at Hunter.

Burns, blisters and cuts covered a quarter of his back. The scar she'd explored during their week together remained, but he'd added several in less than two years.

With a deep inhale, she plunged the rag into the water. Inch by inch she cleaned the wounds. Each time she touched a new section, she braced herself for a curse or a shout, but Hunter didn't make a sound.

She hesitated at the torn flesh under his shoulder blade. Should she dig into the hole or just flush it? Erin couldn't stop the worry from rising in her throat. "The bullet's still inside, isn't it?"

"Nothing exited out the front," Hunter said through gritted teeth.

Her heart lurched at the pain lacing his voice. She didn't want to hurt him, but she didn't have a choice.

"How does it look?" he asked.

She leaned down and studied the hole. "Blood is seeping, but it's only a trickle. The edges are clean."

"Okay."

Taking a deep breath, she pressed around the hole. "Not okay. I'm not a medical doctor. The only training I've got is cleaning up Brandon's scrapes and scratches from his forays into learning to walk. You've got a bullet inside you."

"Yeah, I know. It'll keep. Put some antibiotic ointment on it for now."

Really? Granted, she didn't have that much experience, but were all men as nonchalant about being shot or was this just a Hunter thing?

She applied the cream to the puncture wound and to the burns and scrapes on his shoulders, then dug through the first-aid kid and bandaged the most vulnerable spots.

"That's the best I can do."

Hunter shifted his body. "Thanks. You did great."

"What about the bullet?"

He grimaced. "I hadn't wanted to bring anybody else in, but I can't afford to be out of it, and bullet wounds are notorious for getting infected."

Gingerly, he rolled to his side and sat up.

He slipped a phone from his pants pocket and pressed a code into the keys, then placed the phone against his ear.

"Fabiano."

Thank God the medic had answered. "It's Hunter."

"What the hell's going on? There are rumors everywhere. Some say you've gone AWOL. Some suggest PTSD, or even rogue."

Hunter stilled. "What are you talking about?" This wasn't part of the plan.

Something tugged at Hunter's pants. He glanced down, and his son's mischievous smile grinned up at him. His heart overflowing, Hunter held out his finger and Brandon grabbed hold, squeezing tight, standing up, if not a bit wobbly. The little guy had quite the grip. He tugged Hunter's finger into his mouth and started chewing.

"Look, I don't know what you're into, bud," Doc said, "but it's hitting the fan here. I've never seen the place so chaotic."

"I need your help." Hunter rubbed his temple. "And I want you to keep Leona out of it."

She'd be furious, but Doc's information made the decision easy. Hunter would do everything in his power to keep Leona from coming to him. First, she hadn't been in the field in years; second, her husband would probably take out a hit on Hunter if he involved Leona in something that was looking more and more like a cluster of trouble.

"What are you into, Hunter?"

"She's risked enough for me. I can't let her do more."

"You know I'm there. What's wrong?" Doc barked the question.

"I've got a slug in my back. Bring a medical-surgical kit and keep yourself under the radar."

"How bad?"

Hunter shifted his shoulder. If the bullet had hit his lungs or anything vital, he'd already be dead. Still, he couldn't afford to take any chances. He didn't know how long it would take to get Erin and Brandon to safety. He couldn't chance any more complications. "I haven't bled out, so that's good, right?"

Doc let out a violent curse. "Where are you?"

"Are we secure?"

Doc paused. Hunter listened for the clicks indicating his teammate had encrypted the call.

Hunter rattled off the coordinates. "You'll need a boat."

"Don't die on me until I get there."

"I'll try to avoid it," Hunter said, and smiled down at his son.

Brandon let out a loud laugh, the giggle echoing through the room.

"Was that a baby?" Doc asked, his tone shocked.

"Maybe. Just get here."

"You must have some story to tell. I'm in Virginia. I'll be there as soon as I can."

"Keep it low profile. It's more important than anything I've ever asked." Brandon grabbed Hunter's leg and hugged him. Hunter couldn't stop his eyes from burning as he touched his little boy's hair. He cleared his throat. "You get me?"

"We're a team. When have I ever let you down?"

Never. And that wouldn't change.

Hunter ended the call and met Erin's gaze. "Help is on the way."

"So you say."

She paced back and forth. "Look, I'm glad you're not dying, but I don't understand any of this. What are we doing here? Why can't I just take you to a hospital? Those guys who tried to kill us are dead now."

"They're not the only ones after you, Erin. I thought you'd accepted that."

"Why should I believe anything you've said to me? I'm barely processing that the man who abandoned me in Santorini whom I had finally gotten over isn't the man sitting on that bed just three feet away with a bullet in his back."

"I'm sorry that this happened to you, but the danger hasn't ended. Not yet."

She raised her hand. "Look, *Hunter*—if that's your real name. I'm stuck in the middle of a swamp with our one-year-old son, waiting for some unknown doctor to dig a bullet out of you, and you tell me I'm still in trouble." Erin let out a long, slow breath. "You know something? I realized when I called your so-called company and they'd never heard of you that you were a liar. I've accepted that. Now I realize not only are you a liar, but your life is a lie. And I don't know if I can ever trust you. About anything."

She scooped up Brandon, stalked to the door, shoved aside the chair and slammed outside. Hunter stood there for a moment. Great. What was he supposed to do now? How could he make her understand?

Truth was, he couldn't. Not without revealing more than he'd ever intended.

"What a mess."

He had to tell Erin just enough to scare the hell out of

her and make her embrace his plans for her and Brandon, without giving her enough information that she'd end up expendable.

"How am I supposed to convince her to do this?" he said to the empty room.

It wasn't every day you asked someone to give up her life, her dreams…everything.

The trill of the cicadas outside grew, and the underlying cackle of a heron pierced through the noise. A shriek of laughter sounded from outside, cutting through the chattering of the birds, but the joy didn't make Hunter smile. It just opened the scar where his heart had been.

"Brandon, no," Erin screamed.

Hunter leaped to his feet and raced to the door. He slammed outside. In the dim light, a blunt-nosed alligator at least fifteen feet long hissed at Erin.

She'd climbed onto the porch rail, her face white, with Brandon in her grasp.

The prehistoric beast opened his mouth, looking at them like a snack. It lunged and snapped. Hunter leaped between Erin and the jaws of the beast.

"Make noise," he shouted at Erin.

She shouted and banged a stick on the porch railings. Brandon squealed, his little forehead furrowed, unsure if this was supposed to be fun.

"Where did it come from?" Hunter shouted.

The alligator lunged at them. Hunter narrowed his gaze. He could poke the gator's eyes, but he didn't want to get in a wrestling match so close to the water. The huge animal could drag him into a death roll way too easily.

"We were about ten yards from the east side of the porch," Erin said, her voice shaking.

Hunter glanced in that direction. Sure enough, nestled in a small area near the water, he caught sight of the tops of three eggs. "Get inside," he shouted. "She's defending her eggs."

Erin backed toward the door slowly and disappeared with Brandon into the shack.

Hunter slipped between the slots on the porch toward the eggs. The gator followed, her mouth wide. He paused near the nest. The alligator scrambled at him, its movements jerky and fast, but intent.

"Okay, Mama. I'm not planning to hurt your babies."

He sprinted around the backside of the shack, the gator behind him. He'd put some distance between him and the monster jaws when his foot sank into the swamp.

The animal closed in.

Ten feet, five feet. Hunter tugged his foot free. The alligator snapped. Too close. He squinted in the faint light and grabbed a stick. With a quick move, Hunter jabbed at the animal's eyes.

The move stunned the beast. It backed away, then stilled. Hunter didn't hesitate. He sprinted around the building.

Once out of the alligator's line sight, he eased toward the front of the house, quiet so as not to attract the animal's attention. Gators had excellent hearing.

As the final rays of sun vanished, the alligator grunted several times, hissed and, through the night, returned to her nest and circled, lying in wait.

Hunter's movements silent, he opened the door, walked in, then barricaded his little family inside.

Erin sat at the kitchen table, shaking, Brandon securely in her arms.

"She was protecting her nest," Hunter said, studying her pale face. "Are you both okay?"

She cuddled her son. "I've been kidnapped by a man

who I slept with but didn't know his name and trapped inside a shack by a prehistoric reptile. What do you think?"

"Not your usual day, huh?" Hunter tried to smile.

"Thank you," she said. "Even if it's your fault we almost got eaten."

Hunter didn't want to admit how scared he'd been, seeing Erin and his son facing the beast. She could have plucked Brandon in one bite.

He sank into a chair at the table, his legs shaking. "We'll just stay inside."

"How long?" Erin asked. "I'm assuming you have a plan. What is it? When do I get my life back?"

Hunter leaned forward. "I'm sorry, Erin. You don't."

Chapter Five

The roar of swamp sounds pelted Erin's ears. She couldn't have heard Hunter right.

"Say that again," she whispered.

"I'm sorry, Erin. You don't get your life back." Hunter leaned forward in his chair. "I wish there was some way to make it happen, but—"

Erin had never been more thankful to be sitting down. Her arms weakened. She set Brandon at her feet. He crawled across the floor toward the duffel bag, tugging on the secure straps.

"Why? What did I do?"

"You're brilliant."

She leaned back in her chair. "That doesn't make any sense."

"You saw your prototype as a way to affect small groups of cells, deliver radiation directly to cancer tumors and maybe as a way to treat not only cancer, but other types of diseases."

She nodded and the rush of excitement sent a tingle through her body. She gripped his arm. "It works, Hunter. You don't understand. All the preliminary tests have worked. The treatment could save lives."

"Others see your cure as the perfect assassination tool. Efficient, undetectable, untraceable."

Erin shook her head. No. This was wrong. It couldn't be true.

Hunter let out a long, slow breath. "There are men out there who have made killing their means to an end. Your invention is the perfect means. They want it."

Erin sagged in her chair. She could see the truth on Hunter's face. "Can't you stop them? You or the CIA or whoever you work for?"

Hunter squirmed. "They know about your research. They won't stop until they have the technology, understand it and can duplicate it."

This couldn't be happening. The flicker of the kerosene lamp in the corner of the room bathed the shack in pale light. She rose and paced back and forth. "It's not that easy. You need special material, special equipment that's not at your standard hardware store. I could destroy the prototype. I have it—"

"In your laptop bag. I know."

Erin whirled to face him. "How—?"

"I'm very good at my job. And there are others who are even better. Unfortunately for you, they're on the wrong side. Whether or not the prototype exists doesn't matter. They want your brain—and your skills. And they'll use anyone to get you." He stared right at their son.

Insides trembling, Erin picked up Brandon. She snuggled her son closer. He grabbed her nose and she looked into his innocent eyes. There had to be a way out of this. She turned to Hunter. "What can I do?"

"The men who almost kidnapped you today set it up so that the police think you're dead. Soon enough the news will hit." Hunter paused, then met her gaze. "I want you both to stay dead. Permanently."

At the stark words, Erin's knees trembled. She shook her head. "No. I can't. I have plans. For me, for Brandon."

Hunter crossed to her and reached to cup her cheek. She shrank away from his touch.

He backed off and she relaxed just a bit. "I know it's a lot to take in," he said. "If I could come up with any other choice, believe me, I would. I want both of you to be safe and happy."

"Then leave us alone," she whispered. "Make this go away."

"That's not possible." Hunter paused. "Look, I need to rinse off the grime and change out of these clothes. It'll give you time to come to terms with what has to happen."

Erin couldn't feel anything. How had this happened? How had her dreams turned her world into a nightmare?

Hunter touched her arm. She didn't even have the energy to pull away.

"I won't be long," he said, gathering a shaving kit and a set of clothes from the duffel. He snagged a water bottle from the refrigerator and disappeared into the bathroom.

She couldn't stop a tear from running down her face.

"Mama?" Brandon's lip quivered. He patted her cheek.

"Oh, cutie, what have I done to both of us?"

HUNTER CLOSED THE DOOR TO THE bathroom behind him, leaving a shell-shocked Erin alone with her thoughts. He hated that bewildered expression on her face. The stench of failure soured his mouth, but he couldn't come up with another option for her. Or for him.

He took several swigs of water, then unzipped the leather pouch. He swallowed three ibuprofens, unbuttoned his pants and slipped them off over his muddy shoes. The movement pulled at his wounds. His body felt disconnected from his head. He guzzled down another drink, then turned his back toward the cheap mirror hanging over the sink.

A small whistle escaped as he surveyed the damage. Erin had done a good job with the dressings, but his back was a mess. He shifted his shoulder, testing it. Sharp pain radiated out. His head spun.

He grabbed hold of the sink to steady himself. That bullet needed to come out. Soon. He looked longingly at the showerhead. What he wouldn't give to have the water beating down on his back, easing away the tension, not of the pain, but of facing Erin's palpable disappointment.

Without a choice, he stepped into the tub and cleaned himself the best he could. The bandages didn't need to get wet.

By the time he had dressed, his head had begun pounding again. He stepped into the main room of the darkened shack. Erin stood at the stove, stirring a pot, a now-clean Brandon at her feet. The fragrance of chicken soup wafted through the room, and Hunter's mouth watered.

She glanced over her shoulder. "You don't look so good."

He ran his fingers through his dark, wet hair. "I'm clean."

"How bad is it?" she asked. "Really."

"I'll survive until Doc gets here."

She set a bowl of steaming chicken and noodles in front of him, then took out a box of crackers. "Maybe this will help," she muttered, avoiding his gaze.

Hunter sat down. With each spoonful, he studied her stiff back. She set a jar of baby food in a pan of simmering water for several minutes but didn't turn around. She tested the baby food, then let it heat some more.

He couldn't take the silence. "What are you thinking?"

She didn't budge. "That I want to wake up in the morning and have this day to never have happened."

Brandon crawled over to him and placed his small hands

on Hunter's knee. He touched the baby's hand. Hunter could understand Erin's feelings, but he couldn't agree. While every moment he spent with them made him want more, how could he regret any time spent with his son?

Hunter ruffled the boy's head. "How you doin', sport?"

With a grip Hunter could barely fathom, Brandon pressed himself to his feet, arms solid but legs unsteady.

"Brandon stood up. By himself." An inordinate pride rushed through Hunter. "Isn't he young for that?"

At his words, Erin turned, her eyes shining with love when she watched their son. She grinned for the first time since Hunter had walked through the front door of her house. "He's right on track," Erin said. "According to research, he'll start walking between eleven and fourteen months."

"Hear that, sport? You're doing great." Hunter took a cracker and downed it.

At the move, Brandon's eyes widened and he reached his hands up. "Yum. Yum…yum…yum."

A strange dread clamped around Hunter at his son's eager expression. "What does he want?"

"Don't panic. He's just hungry." Erin emptied the baby food into a bowl. "Come on, cutie. Ready to eat?"

At his mother's questions, Brandon tried to whirl around. He almost made it. He wobbled, then sat down. Hard. Hunter bit back a curse and leaned over. "Brandon! Are you okay?"

The boy's face screwed up, and Hunter's heart raced. Was his son going to cry? The boy didn't get the chance. Erin scooped him up and kissed his belly. "Oopsie-daisy. Did you fall down?"

The almost-cry turned into giggles. With an efficient move, she sat down and plopped Brandon in her lap. "Let's get you a full tummy and put you to bed."

His meal forgotten, Hunter couldn't take his eyes off the image of Erin and their son. Her tenderness, her care, the utter devotion on her face tugged at something deep within him he could barely define. He wanted to hold his son; he wanted to take care of them both. He wanted a life. With Erin.

The reality of their situation hurt Hunter's heart. Maybe Erin had been right in her wish. Would it have been better to never have experienced today?

Brandon spit out some of the horrid-looking puce food. She laughed and wiped his face, then met Hunter's gaze over Brandon's head. Her expression softened a bit. "Do you want to feed him?"

Being in the thick of a firefight hadn't made his heart race as fast as her question. "I don't—"

She didn't let him finish, just rose and handed him the baby. Brandon's lips stuck out, and he reached for his mother.

"He doesn't want me." Hunter couldn't stop the disappointment that shadowed his spirit at the rejection.

"It's all about dinner," Erin said. "Be careful. The spoon is bigger than he's used to."

Hunter balanced his son on his lap. He took a small amount of the unappetizing dinner and offered it up with a horrified fascination. Shockingly, the baby sucked in the puree and grinned, opening his mouth wide for a disgusting view. "Better you than me, sport."

With each spoonful, Hunter got a bit more comfortable. Even when Brandon grabbed Hunter's chin with sticky fingers, he couldn't stop smiling. He met Erin's gaze. "Thank you."

The simple words elicited a tender smile from Erin. Hunter took the gift for what is was, a temporary reprieve.

Soon enough reality would set in, but for now the world was good.

Erin studied them both and tugged at her ruined clothes. "Will you be okay with him if I take a shower?"

"Of course. How hard can it be?"

She quirked a brow, but nodded and vanished into the bathroom with the clothes they'd purchased earlier in the day. The shower turned on and Hunter dug into one last spoon of Brandon's dinner. "We're all alone, sport. We can handle it, right?"

Brandon smacked his lips and finished up his dinner.

"Your mommy is one tough cookie. Don't tell her this, but I'd give anything to run away with you guys." He took the damp rag Erin had left him and wiped Brandon's face. His son's forehead crinkled. "I know, I know. But the women like guys without food stuck to their face. Remember that."

Brandon reached for the crackers and Hunter grabbed one and placed it in his son's hand. He chewed on the cracker, making a gooey mess, and leaned back against Hunter's chest.

A thickness closed his throat. "How am I going to let you go, sport? I didn't have a dad, so I don't know how to be one, but I'd do my best to teach you right from wrong. And how to throw a football like a guy, not a girl."

Brandon stuffed his fist in his mouth and burrowed deeper into the crook of Hunter's arm. The baby's eyes drooped. Hunter laid his lips on his son's hair and closed his eyes, taking in the baby scent, committing each touch and smell to memory. This moment would have to last him a very long time.

An irritating ring interrupted Hunter's bittersweet thoughts. Brandon's eyelids flew open. His tiny mouth frowned. He sat up and looked around, and gripped Hunter's hand hard.

With a quick tug, Hunter pulled the phone from his pocket and stared at the screen.

Leona.

He should have known, but after what Doc had said, Hunter didn't want Leona anywhere near this situation. He had to protect her almost as much as he had to protect his family. He had to cut her off, give her plausible deniability until he discovered exactly what was going on. He powered off the phone and stuffed it back into his pocket.

He just prayed she understood the message and backed off.

Brandon squirmed in Hunter's lap, frantically searching the room. The baby's eyes filled with tears. He reached out his arms and clasped Hunter's fist over and over again. "Mama. Mama…Mama…Mama."

Hunter jiggled the boy. "It's okay, sport. I'm here."

Brandon opened his mouth and let out a high-pitched, eardrum-bursting cry.

Frantic, Hunter stood, ignoring the agony piercing his shoulder. He held his son, bounced him and whispered to him. He tried everything. His goofy face only made Brandon cry louder. Crazy voices scared him. Bribery didn't work.

He could imagine what his teammates or Leona would say if they'd witnessed his utter incompetence.

Finally, when the hiccups took over and huge tears slid down Brandon's cheeks, Hunter couldn't stand it any longer. He knocked on the bathroom door.

The sound of water pounding down didn't stop, and neither did Brandon's screams. Out of options, Hunter turned the doorknob slowly and pushed open the bathroom door.

He froze. Erin's silhouette arched beneath the spray.

Through the white curtain he could see the outline of each and every curve. He should have looked away, but he couldn't. She tilted her neck and let the waterfall of water wash over her head.

She was more beautiful and sensual than he remembered. Her breasts were a bit fuller than they'd been on Santorini, and her curves made his mouth dry with want.

"Your mommy is hot, sport," he whispered to Brandon, who had quit screaming at least. The baby leaned toward the shower. Clearly, he knew his mother.

Erin bent down, flipped off the water and thrust the shower curtain aside.

Her eyes widened. Hunter's brain went numb.

She grabbed the towel on the edge of the sink and whipped it around her body. "What are you doing?"

"Brandon wouldn't stop crying," Hunter said, barely able to speak. Lame, but his blood had left his brain, pooling low in his belly. His body thrummed with awareness that he shouldn't feel, couldn't feel.

He stood his ground when his entire being urged him to pull her into his arms. Silence reigned between them. Seconds passed, and memories slid over Hunter of more than one shared shower in an island paradise.

Erin's cheeks flushed; her lips parted and her tongue bathed her mouth. She remembered.

Oh, boy.

Just one step, and he could kiss her. He leaned forward.

"Mama." Brandon tilted his head and looked at Erin with a grin.

The moment was gone.

Erin tucked the towel more tightly around her, unwilling to meet his gaze. "Yeah, he seems very upset."

"He *was* crying," Hunter protested.

"Since he's okay now, could you please let me get dressed?"

He couldn't leave the room fast enough and closed the door behind him. "Thanks a lot, sport. Now she thinks I'm a pervert."

A few minutes later, Erin reentered dressed in a T-shirt and jeans. She held out her arms. Reluctantly, Hunter handed over Brandon. The baby tucked his head against his mother's shoulder and closed his eyes.

"Why wouldn't he do that for me?" Hunter asked.

She stroked her son's back. "Because I'm his mom." Her gaze shifted from the bed to Hunter. "He needs sleep."

"Put him on the bed," Hunter said. "I'll sit up tonight. I'm not tired."

"Liar."

Hunter quirked a smile. "Maybe, but I need to check the perimeter. Just in case."

After an uneventful security check around the cabin, and a small salute to the mama gator, Hunter returned to the shack. Erin had curled up with Brandon. He lay passed out with his fist in his mouth.

With a resigned sigh, Hunter grabbed a couple of blankets from the armoire and threw them on the floor.

"Don't," Erin whispered. "There's room for all of us."

Hunter hesitated.

"You need your rest," she added, toying with the fine black hair on Brandon's forehead.

"He's amazing, Erin. You're a good mother."

Could she hear the yearning lacing his voice? God, he hoped not.

"Brandon makes it easy. He has so much joy inside."

"I wish…" Hunter couldn't complete the thought. He doused the lamp, and the room turned mostly dark, save small slivers of moonlight filtering through the wooden shutters.

"Me, too." She tucked Brandon in closer. "I thought we had something special."

Hunter eased his face down onto the bed. His entire body hurt; his back ached; his throat was scratchy. And yet he couldn't drift off to sleep. He couldn't stop from breathing in the scent of both of them. What he wouldn't give to have them part of his life.

Brandon's small snores purred, and soon Erin's soft breathing grew steady. Their lives together could have been special.

Hunter had even considered leaving the organization. He'd thrown out a few hints to the general. The man had been sympathetic but clear. Could Hunter live with the consequences if his past followed him and his family were caught in the cross fire?

Easy answer. Hunter would do anything to keep Erin and Brandon safe. Even let them go.

Trouble was, what had been a lonely future had turned bleaker than he had ever imagined. He let his finger slide down Brandon's cheek and hover over Erin's hand.

Now he knew what he'd be missing.

THEY'D PUT TERENCE IN A private room. Probably so he wouldn't scare the other patients.

He pressed his hand against the patch over the socket where his eye had been. They'd removed it. The doctors said he could be fitted with a glass eye.

Son of a bitch.

He breathed in. The smell of antiseptic overwhelmed him.

They'd told him how lucky he'd been, that his burns

would heal eventually, and so would his body. With enough surgery his appearance would improve.

He might have to get a Phantom of the Opera mask. He didn't really care about his looks. He'd have to learn to live without an eye, though. He didn't mind that much, except it made him vulnerable.

"Mr. Mahew," a quiet voice whispered from his bedside. Just like that.

Terence hadn't seen the guy coming. Normally, his peripheral vision would have warned him.

The man wore a long white coat, but when Terence glanced at his shoes—handmade, spit-and-polish black— nausea bubbled in Terence's belly. His hand reached under his pillow. His weapon wasn't there.

He felt on the bedside table. A plastic knife. He could make do.

"What do you want?" he asked.

"Is that any way to treat your customer?" the man asked.

Terence stared up the man. "You're not the man I made a deal with. Wrong voice."

"He doesn't take out the garbage, Mr. Mahew. You failed to deliver on your assignment. My employer is not pleased."

Terence could see the next few minutes as surely as if he were watching a movie.

Not a good ending, but Terence Mahew wasn't a man who would go down without a fight.

Eyeing his enemy, he shifted so he could maneuver better in the bed.

"I'm out of it. I quit," Terence said, buying as much time as he could.

"Oh, I agree. The money has been removed from your account, but we have unfinished business."

The man leaned over Terence's bedside, a cold smile on his face.

Terence clutched the plastic knife. In one thrust he stabbed the weapon at the man's eye. His opponent dodged in a blinding-fast move. He rested his palm under Terence's nose.

"You know I can kill you." he said. "I will kill you. Failure is not an option."

Terence couldn't look away from the man's deadly gaze. His eyes were cold, soulless.

The truth sucked the energy from Terence. He was dead.

The man smiled.

Then his eyes rolled back into his head.

Blood poured from a small hole on the man's neck. He sagged to the floor.

Terence gaped at his second visitor.

A man in a perfectly pressed suit tucked a metal skewer into his pocket. Several crew-cut men filed into the hospital room and wrapped the body in plastic, cleaning up the mess with scary precision. "Terence Mahew?"

He nodded, his mouth gaping.

He'd almost wet himself at the efficiency of this man's move, and after killing over a hundred people in his lifetime, being in combat, watching his buddies die, that said something.

"My name is Padgett. You're wanted in Virginia. We would like to have a word with you about your—" he glanced at the dead body "—former employers."

He tossed Terence some sweats. "Get dressed if you want to live another day."

ERIN SAT IN THE KITCHEN CHAIR and tucked her knees into her chest. The afternoon sun filtered through the window's slats. She'd convinced Hunter to lie down with Brandon for his nap on the auspices that he wouldn't sleep. She'd had an ulterior motive, though. Since this morning, Hunter's cheeks had grown flushed, and he'd turned an ugly shade of gray when Brandon accidently hit his back.

She glanced at the door for the umpteenth time. It had been twenty-four hours since he'd been shot, and Hunter had refused to let her look under the bandages. He'd said Doc would be here soon.

Unable to sit still a second longer, Erin crossed the room. She studied Hunter's features. He didn't look comfortable. A frown line marred his forehead; perspiration had broken through.

She laid a hand on his cheek.

Too hot.

"Oh, Hunter."

The day had started out surreal. Despite feeling under par, he'd responded to Brandon's every move. Her son had taken to Hunter faster than a gamma ray. Maybe it was a guy thing to connect at the speed of light, but they seemed to speak the same language.

From the bed, Brandon blinked up at her and smiled. He patted Hunter on the chest. Hunter groaned softly. Brandon frowned at his daddy. Erin could see the intent on her son's face. She quickly picked him up and carried him to a makeshift playpen in the middle of the living room. "Daddy's not feeling good. Why don't you play with Socky?" Kneeling down, she handed him his puppet.

Brandon squealed and threw the sock at her. She squatted down to pick up the toy. He grinned at her, the look in his eyes merry with mischievousness.

So like the man she'd met on Santorini.

"You did that on purpose."

He grinned wider.

She returned the toy and tousled the hair. "Your daddy's getting sick. If help doesn't come soon, we have to get him to the hospital. No matter what he says. He needs antibiotics."

Brandon patted her face and blew some bubbles at her. She smiled, and then a slight sound wafted from outside—a rumbling she recognized.

Erin stilled. She glanced at the gun Hunter had placed on top of the armoire earlier. She kissed the top of her son's head. "Be good."

She chanced a glance out the shack's window.

Another airboat sped up the narrow waterway. A man with light brown hair and tanned skin drove the boat. No question he knew where he was headed. The vehicle slowed. His body on alert, the man's intensity reminded her of Hunter. He swerved to the dock.

Erin straightened her shoulders, cracked open the door and gripped the weapon tight. She pointed it directly at the man's head, telling herself over and over again not to let her hand shake. She couldn't show vulnerability. Not until she knew his identity. "Who are you?" she asked, her voice calm.

He cocked his head at the handgun.

"Tell me your name," she ordered again.

"Doc," he said. "You the mom of the baby I heard laughing on the phone?"

She let out a slow, deep breath and lowered her weapon. Finally. "Erin Jamison. It took you long enough to get here."

"Erin Jamison? From Pensacola?" His eyes narrowed, and he let out a loud curse. "What the hell has that idiot got himself into this time?" He grabbed a bag and jumped onto the pier. "Where is he?"

"Inside. He's developed a fever." Strange. She'd never seen this man. How did he know her name?

An unsettling wave washed through her belly. She kept the gun in her hand and followed Doc inside to Hunter's bedside. Brandon jabbered at the new intruder. The visitor took one look at her son, then stared down at Hunter. "Dude, when you complicate things, you do a hell of a job." He turned to Erin. "Where's he hurt?"

"I'm not invisible," Hunter groused.

"Clay, your favorite teammate is here."

Hunter opened his eyes and frowned. "Don't bother, she knows my real name."

Doc lifted an eyebrow. "Really?"

"Long story." Hunter shifted and winced.

"I'd guess so after seeing that little miniature you. You look like you've been dragged through the swamp by an alligator. Let's have a gander at the damage."

"I'll make it simple," Hunter said, and flipped onto his stomach. "Bullet under my shoulder blade, a few burns. Just patch me up, give me some antibiotics and forget you ever saw us."

Doc removed the bandage under Hunter's scapula. His mouth screwed up. "So glad you've got a medical degree now. You dress this?" he asked Erin.

She bit her lip and nodded.

"Good job, but the bullet needs to come out."

"Didn't I just say that?" Hunter groused.

The medic pulled a sealed surgical kit out of a small bag. He dug inside. "Shut up and swallow this pill."

Hunter downed it. "What did you give me?"

"Pain pill. You're going to need it."

"Damn it, Doc. I need to be alert."

"You need sleep more." Doc laid out a sterile pack, complete with a scalpel, forceps and sutures. "Have you got a strong stomach, Dr. Jamison? I could use a second set of hands if your baby is occupied."

She couldn't let Hunter down. No matter what he'd done in the past, he'd taken that bullet to save them. "Whatever you need."

He gave her an approving nod. "Let's wash up."

They scrubbed and slipped on surgical gloves. Doc took a syringe and filled it. She couldn't help the shiver.

"Lidocaine. It'll numb the area." He placed his hand on Hunter's back. "You ready, bud?"

"Just get it done," Hunter said.

After Doc plunged the anesthetic just under Hunter's skin, he pressed on the area. "You feel anything?"

"Just pressure."

"Good." Using a scalpel, Doc made a quick incision on either side of the bullet hole.

Erin didn't have time to think. She followed Doc's orders and within seconds the medic explored the hole with forceps. A low moan escaped Hunter. Erin bit her lip and shifted her back in sympathy.

"Almost there. Hang on." Doc maneuvered the instrument, then smiled. "Got it." He pulled out a slug and dropped it into the kit. "Round one accomplished. Now we have to clean these wounds."

They worked to cleanse the rest of Hunter's back, treat the wounds with silver nitrate cream and reapply the bandages.

"Okay. We're done."

"Thank God," Hunter said with a groan.

Erin's knees shook. She glanced over at Brandon. Her son had quiet tears rolling down his face, his thumb stuffed in his mouth as he looked at his daddy.

"I know how you feel, cutie," Erin said softly, blinking back the burning in her eyes. She glanced at Doc. "Is he going to be okay?"

"I'm fine," Hunter interjected.

Doc smiled and pulled out another syringe. He pushed down Hunter's pants, revealing a very muscular butt, then stabbed him. "This should jump-start the healing. I'll leave a week's worth of pills. Take them or you'll ruin my good work."

Relief filtered through Erin. She liked Doc's tone. Hunter really was going to be okay.

Their patient glared at Doc, though. "You enjoyed showing my bare hind end way too much."

"Yeah, I did." The smile creased, then left Doc's face. "I'm glad it wasn't worse. It could have been."

"Are you a doctor?" she asked.

"Hardly. I learned the skill out of necessity, and not always with a good outcome."

Something about Doc's tense shoulders made her nervous. The two men met gazes, and the communication between them made Erin quiver. Doc might be a healer, but he had Hunter's edge. That indefinable quality that said he would do whatever it took, no matter the cost.

"Protect them," Hunter said, his voice slurring just a bit, and then he closed his eyes.

Erin knelt beside the bed and pushed away the hair from Hunter's forehead. Something she might never have done when he was awake. It was safer to her heart without his knowing brown eyes searing through her. "He's really going to be okay?"

She lifted her lashes, ignoring the slight dampness on their tips.

The medic's expression gentled. "By tomorrow he'll be a new man. You'll never know this happened."

Erin bit her lip. "And you're staying?"

"Oh, yeah. You have at least three groups of people looking for you. Until Hunter regains consciousness, Dr. Jamison, I'm your bodyguard."

Chapter Six

The pulsing surf of Santorini sounded in Hunter's ear. The black beaches of the volcanic island gleamed against the turquoise sea. The woman across from him smiled, her eyes guileless, her expression open and honest.

Everything he wasn't.

The backdrop of the ocean framed her blond hair. Several strands had escaped the sophisticated knot. He missed the flowing blond locks he'd seen when they'd first met. Now his fingers itched to release the captured tresses so they'd once again bathe her shoulders.

He prayed his gaze didn't telegraph half of what he wanted from Erin. Every instinct within him shouted that her innocence was real, evoking a protective feeling that he hadn't felt since his mom had gotten so sick.

He couldn't stop staring at her. From the amazingly long lashes surrounding her emerald eyes, to the blush staining her cheeks, to the fullness of her lips. He wanted to hold Erin in his arms and fold her close. He wanted to touch her in ways no man had. He wanted her to cry out his name.

Erin took a shuddering breath and lowered her gaze. She must have recognized his want. God, she was beautiful with this naive, hopeful air he'd never experienced.

If only he could wash away the stains of everything he had done.

She cleared her throat. "Why did you choose Santorini, Clay?"

Right. Clay. Not Hunter. Not in this place.

Her gaze begged him to take their conversation somewhere safe. He reined in his desire as best he could. He didn't want to scare her, but this primal force inside drew him. He scooted his chair a bit closer.

"I needed a vacation. My last job was…brutal."

More than she would ever know. Blood, bullets, betrayal. Not from his team. Never from them. From the moment General Miller had tapped him directly out of his Special Ops training, the team had become his family. He would sacrifice everything for each of them, and he had no doubt they would do the same, but year after year the enemy became less clear. Informants turned on them; insiders changed loyalty more often than he changed socks. Hunter was so tired of the game. He still believed his organization's work to be critically important, but fatigue gnawed at him from the inside. Bone-jarring, soul-wasting exhaustion.

"I guess the economy has made the consulting business tough," she said, sympathy clouding her expression.

He shifted in his chair, the discomfort unwelcome—and disconcerting. Normally, he wouldn't feel even a twinge of guilt in that minor of a lie, but with Erin his standard operating procedures felt wrong. He crumbled the napkin in his lap. The woman across from him was perfection. Better than he deserved. She took a sip of white wine, but instead of getting up and leaving, he reached for her hand.

She studied his fingers enveloping hers, but she didn't pull away. Something inside Hunter swelled. She wanted him, too. He could feel it.

"Tell me more about your research," he prompted, desperate to shift his focus from her extremely kissable lips.

Her eyes lit up with excitement. He didn't understand half of the technical terms she used, but as each minute passed his belly twisted. When she mentioned radioactive isotopes and targeted exposures, his neck tightened. He could see the Departments of Defense and Homeland Security salivating at the potential weaponization for her nanosized robot. And the terrorists—they'd pay a fortune.

Did she understand the implications of her research? He wanted to tell her to stop, to use her talents somewhere else, but he didn't want to dim the energy pulsing from her entire body. She saw the cure for cancer, treatment for epilepsy, healing of severed nerves.

Erin saw the good.

Hunter saw only the destruction.

Two opposites. She was brilliant, innovative, a prodigy. He was a homeless high school dropout with a knack for languages and a talent for surveillance and killing the enemy.

Did he need any other reason why they wouldn't work?

"I've never met anyone as brilliant as you are," he said, lacing his fingers through hers, unable to stop himself from touching her.

"Please don't say that," she said, trying to pull her hands away.

He gripped tighter. "Why not?"

She gulped down the rest of her wine. "I don't want to be different. I'm sick of it. I don't want to be the sixteen-year-old college freshman who no one wanted to talk to, or the doctoral student who couldn't go to a bar with her colleagues because she was too young. Or the girl who got passed over for every dance and every party throughout her college career."

With every word, Hunter understood more and more. He tilted her chin up. "Have you ever been on a date before?"

She flushed, her embarrassment obvious. She lifted her chin in defiance. "Of course."

"With someone you wanted?"

"Not really." She sighed. She pushed back from the table and rose, uncertain. "I can't believe I just told you that. I should go."

Hunter stood and blocked her path, toe-to-toe with Erin. Her trembling frame hovered like a hummingbird preparing to flit away.

"Have you ever been kissed?" he asked, his voice a bare whisper over the surf.

She licked her lips and nodded.

"By someone you wanted?" He stroked her cheek.

She shook her head and leaned into his touch. The tension between them had grown thick and real enough to touch.

Hunter intertwined his fingers with hers. She looked up at him with such a trusting gaze she hurt his heart. Erin Jamison couldn't be real.

"I want to kiss you," he said, his words so full of want he barely recognized himself.

Her eyes widened.

"Do you want me?"

She leaned into him. Her lips parted in silent invitation. The patrons in the restaurant faded away.

He closed his eyes and brushed his mouth against hers, gentle and more beautiful, more tender than anything he'd known. He couldn't tell which of them shivered. Perhaps they both did. Her softness parted and he tasted the sweetness, the invitation in each caress.

Something strong and tight clamped around his heart. Stunned, he lifted his head. Her green eyes had turned foggy.

She didn't speak. She just stared into his eyes.

He couldn't rip himself from the spell she cast onto him.

"Come with me," he said, his voice shaking with longing. He dropped a wad of cash on the table and held out his hand, praying she would agree, hoping she wouldn't run the other way.

She squeezed his hand, not letting him go.

He shoved aside his better judgment. He couldn't resist her, even though he knew he should. Erin's light would bathe him in warmth. He could feel it. For one night, he would experience what he'd never thought he could find.

She plastered her body against him, gripping his arm tight. "This is crazy," she whispered. "I don't do things like this, Clay."

"Neither do I," he whispered. And for once his words weren't a lie.

Hunter led her onto the beach toward the bungalow he'd rented for the week. The waves rolled in close to them. He turned her into his arms. "Last chance, Erin. I can take you back to your room, but if we go inside, I won't be able to resist touching you. Are you ready for that?"

She smiled and lifted her hands to his chest. "I came here to experience life for the first time. I want you to be my teacher."

She pressed her mouth to his. He didn't hesitate. He scooped her into his arms.

He might regret ignoring his conscience, but for tonight he would hold heaven in his arms.

HUNTER DIDN'T KNOW WHAT FELT worse, the fog in his brain or the daylight streaming in and assaulting his vision. He squeezed his eyelids shut and let out a groan.

A gentle hand pressed against his forehead.

"Erin—" he whispered.

"Just don't try to kiss me, bud."

Hunter's eyelids flew open and took in Doc's unshaven features. The man had saved his life more than once. He'd have to start a tab, and when Hunter finally paid Doc, the price would be steep.

His gaze scanned the room. Empty. His shoulders tensed and his pulse raced. "Where's Erin?"

"In the bathroom bathing the kid." Doc propped one combat boot on his leg. "The baby's yours?"

"Couldn't you tell?"

"He's cuter than you, but I would have recognized that crazy hairstyle anywhere. I always thought you used gel to get that interesting rooster effect."

The lips of Hunter's mouth tilted up and he rubbed his face. "He's my son, Doc. What the hell am I supposed to do about that?"

"I'm sorry," Doc said quietly. "Do you have a plan?"

"Keep them safe," Hunter said, meeting his friend's gaze. "Even if Erin wasn't a target, you know I can't be part of his life."

"Sucks." Doc nodded slightly. "Does Miller know?"

"No one knows. Except for the lawyer I hired to set up a trust for Brandon. Just in case." Hunter sighed. "And Leona."

Doc rubbed in chin. "You know she and Miller came up together, right?"

"Don't go there, Doc. She'd never let me down. Besides, once I leave this shack, she doesn't know anything about the rest of my plan." Hunter sat up and took inventory of his body. He moved his shoulder. Sore, but bearable. "How long was I out?"

"Twenty-four hours."

"Too long in one place. We need to get out of here. Thanks, Doc. I feel human again."

"Good. You're going to need all your strength. I heard from Daniel."

"How is he?" Hunter asked, his voice low. The operative had been kidnapped and tortured for weeks around Christmas. He'd barely survived.

"It took a good six months, but physically he's mostly healed. Emotionally...I'm not convinced," Doc said. "He asked about you."

"Why? I haven't seen him since we broke him out of that dungeon in Bellevaux."

"He's trying to get reinstated for active duty. He heard your name mentioned in the facility where he goes for his postcaptivity shrink visits."

Hunter shuddered. "I bet he hates those."

"Oh, yeah. But he said someone dropped a hint that you might be suffering some sort of breakdown."

Hunter shoved back the bedding and placed his feet on the floor, testing his balance. He weighed this new information in his mind. "That doesn't make any sense. I'm supposed to be on vacation."

"Look, Hunter, I would argue this is just a snafu except for one thing. Your name has made it on a search list. Someone is looking for you. I had to do some fast talking—and grand theft—to get here. There are suits combing the area for you. Air, bus, train—they're all being watched."

Hunter rose and paced across the floor, a flurry of curses escaping him. "That screws up the next phase of my plan. I wanted to take a small plane to Texas. Logan set me up with the lawyer. He lives in Carder."

"Then what are you going to do?"

"I've got to get rid of Erin and Brandon."

"Are you planning to feed us to the alligator?" Erin

asked, standing in the doorway with a washed and polished Brandon on her hip, her expression frozen and unreadable.

"That's not what I—"

"Da—" His son reached out his arms.

Hunter's knees shook and he stared at the grinning baby.

Doc cleared his throat. "I'm heading outside for a few." He left the room and softly closed them inside.

Brandon squirmed in Erin's arms. "Da…Da…Da," he chortled, stretching out to Hunter.

Reluctantly, she passed the squiggly baby over. Hunter took him and settled his son in the crook of his arm.

"Da!" Brandon grinned.

Hunter worked his throat around the knot that had risen in it. "When—"

She shrugged. "It's an easy word to say." She twisted her fingers in her lap. "What did you mean you have to get rid of me?"

He shoved his hand through his hair. "Look, it's all part of helping you disappear. Erin and Brandon Jamison died in that fire. You no longer exist."

"I've thought about this, Hunter, but I can't believe someone can't help us. The FBI, somebody. I know you're just trying to protect us, but it's not your job. It's mine. I'm glad you're better," she said, "but this is too much. We need to go back to our life."

He could feel the frustration rising within her, but that was nothing compared to his own. How stubborn could one woman be? How could he make her believe him? "Erin, your work makes you valuable," he said, his voice rising. "These men are ruthless. I've known more than one person to just disappear. I refuse to pick up the paper someday and have you and our son another statistic."

"Isn't that what we are already?" Erin challenged.

"But you're safe."

Brandon leaned back and stuck his thumb in his mouth. He lay cradled against Hunter's chest, content and happy. The slight weight stung Hunter's eyes.

This wasn't what he wanted, but it was what had to be.

Hunter put his hand on his son's head. "If I can find you a new life, a new identity, then you have a chance to start over. You can be safe, and no one will ever know. It's the only way."

"But my work, how could I continue it? Long distance?"

"You wouldn't. You are too innovative, too special. They would know. Your new life will have to be completely unrelated. If anyone were to suspect—"

"No more research," Erin said quietly.

"Not as a scientist."

Erin hugged her arms around her body. "I've worked my entire life to succeed at a profession I was born to work, and you're telling me that my career, my dreams are simply gone?"

He leaned forward. "Is your job worth your life? Or our son's?"

THE OPPRESSIVE HUMIDITY CLUNG to every inch of Erin's skin. She tugged the clingy T-shirt she'd bought. She wanted nothing more than an air-conditioned house, her laptop and Brandon. Without Hunter.

"There has to be another way."

Brandon wriggled in Hunter's arms and tugged at his father's nose. He was fascinated by his daddy, just as Erin had been.

For a week she'd believed Clay was absolutely perfect. Hunter was determined to take her life away.

He shoved his hair through his hair. "Look, once you're safe, I'll do everything in my power to figure out some

way for you to come out of hiding, but until we can eliminate the threat, you'll have to stay hidden."

Doc slammed open the door. "We got company. They
found us faster than I thought. At least five coming in on
an airboat. Maybe more."

Hunter glared at Doc. "Someone followed you."

"No way, man. I'm better than that. I told you, they're
canvassing everywhere. It was only a matter of time."

Hunter lifted Brandon and handed him to Erin.

"How much time?" she asked, and clutched her son in
her arms.

"Not much," Doc said.

Hunter opened a secret compartment. He pulled out a
huge weapon and handed one to Doc. He snapped a mag-
azine in the second submachine gun and then tucked a
knife into his boot.

Hunter's jaw tightened, and he slipped two clips into
his vest pocket before handing a pair to Doc. "Let's go."

Erin hugged Brandon close and followed Hunter and
Doc to the door. Hunter glanced out the window and let
out a sharp curse. He yanked the curtains closed.

"They're too close. We'll never make it to the boats,
much less out the inlet in one piece."

She gripped the back of his shirt. "Can we go out back,
across the land?"

Hunter looked at Brandon. "Me and Doc. Maybe. But
we're too far out. With you and the baby, I just don't think
we'll make it."

Doc peeked through the window. "If we're going, it has
to be now. Verify five bogeys," he said.

Hunter's eyes narrowed and Erin shivered at the steely
cold of his expression. "Go out back and around on the
west side of the house. There's a mother gator on the east
side near a clump of trees."

Doc nodded.

"What about me?" Erin asked.

Hunter opened the closet door. "Get in there and don't make a sound." He handed her a revolver. "Hunker down in the closet. If someone breaks in, don't hesitate. Point at the guy's chest and pull the trigger." He flicked on the safety and handed her the weapon.

The roar of an engine moved closer. Erin held Brandon and sank down in the closet. She gripped the gun tight. Hunter gave her a small grin. "Just don't shoot me."

She nodded. "Hunter…be careful."

He winked at her. "Five is nothing. Doc and I can take care of this." He crouched down. "I won't let either of you down. I promise."

He twisted the lock and closed the door.

A few minutes later, Erin heard a loud curse.

"Seven, not five," Doc barked.

A machine gun spit bullets. They thwacked against the wood. Would they come directly through the door? Erin ducked down farther, making herself and Brandon as small a target as possible. Her entire body shook. More gunfire ripped through the air. Brandon whimpered and Erin whispered in his ear.

Glass exploded way too close. A loud crash shook the building. Footsteps thundered at her.

"They got in," Doc yelled.

"Find her," a voice shouted.

There were only two doors to check. The bathroom door slammed open. Shouts sounded from outside, but she couldn't tell who. What if Doc and Hunter couldn't stop them? Two against seven weren't very good odds.

The doorknob shook.

"Gotcha," the voice said.

Erin squeezed the gun tight.

The door smashed in.

Erin didn't hesitate. She pointed the gun at the man's chest and fired. He grunted and fell back. Then groaned.

No blood. He wasn't dead.

Oh, God. Bulletproof vest?

He rolled over, panting.

No. She'd never let him take her.

She had only seconds. She needed another weapon.

Clutching Brandon in her arms, Erin vaulted over the guy with a kick to the head and sprinted into the bathroom. She locked the door but knew the flimsy wood wouldn't protect her for long. A loud curse echoed at her.

Another round of machine-gun fire pelted the air.

Frantically, Erin yanked open the bathroom drawers. She scanned each compartment. A nail file wouldn't cut it. Neither would the long-reach lighter. She opened the medicine cabinet. Shampoo. Toothpaste. A can of deodorant.

A chemical formula flooded through Erin's head.

Deodorant. Aerosol deodorant. Flammable.

The lighter.

It could work.

She grabbed the can and snapped off the top, then thrust Brandon into the bathtub

"It'll be okay, cutie. I promise."

She closed the curtain on him. Seconds later the guy pulverized the door.

She clicked on the flame and pressed down.

The deodorant spewed out the nozzle.

Fire erupted and flew onto the man's chest and face. He shouted and fell back, rolling to douse the flames.

Erin aimed the can at him, her body tense.

Hunter rushed into the room.

Screaming, the guy rolled over and pointed his weapon at Erin.

Hunter didn't hesitate. He pulled the trigger.

The man's head exploded.

OUTSIDE, THE SWAMP HAD GONE eerily silent. Hunter didn't give the man on the floor a second glance. He planted himself between the attacker's body and Erin, and he pulled her shaking body into his arms.

Footsteps pounded on the wood. Hunter twisted slightly, still holding Erin, and raised his weapon at the open door.

A patterned knock sounded.

Hunter lowered his weapon at the signal and Doc walked into the room, his machine gun at the ready.

"They're alligator food," he said, then took in the burned man on the floor, and the spray can in Erin's hand. "Damn, girl. Remind me not to piss you off."

"Oh, God."

Erin dropped the can, covered her mouth and ran into the bathroom. Hunter met Doc's gaze with a grimace.

"I did the same thing," Doc said. "First kill, but don't tell anyone."

"Me, too," Hunter said. "Help me get rid of this. She doesn't need to see it."

They disposed of the body in the swamp. The floating plants churned under the water, and soon the body had been pulled under.

The noises of the swamp had returned to normal by the time they walked back into the shack.

"Can you clean it up?" Hunter asked Doc. "I need to check on her, and we don't have much time. No telling how many know our location."

Doc nodded and Hunter stood just outside the remnants of the bathroom door. He knocked on the doorjamb. "Erin?" He poked his head in.

She was on the bathroom floor, Brandon cradled in her

arms. The baby must have sensed something because he didn't cry, he just patted her arm.

He looked up at Hunter. "Mama."

"I know, sport."

Hunter crouched down. "Erin, we have to go. Can you understand me, sweetie?"

She looked up at him. "I killed him. Burned him to death. How could I do that?"

He gripped her tight. "Listen to me. You did the only thing you could to protect yourself. He would have had no remorse handing you and Brandon over to the terrorists."

She swallowed deeply.

"You done good, Erin." Her scooped her beneath her arm and helped her to her feet. "Now let's get out of here."

She held Brandon close, and Hunter led them across the shack.

She glanced down at the scorched floor. A shiver washed through her, but then she stiffened her back and adjusted their son in her arms.

Man, Erin was one tough woman when she had to be.

Hunter escorted them to the small dock. His gaze swept the area. No body parts that he could see. He kissed her temple. "Will you be okay while I finish packing up?"

Erin took in a deep breath and glanced over at the alligator's nest. The creature gave them a harsh glare, then hunkered down by her eggs. She nodded. "Get us that new identity, Hunter. Brandon has to be safe."

Hunter nodded and returned to the shack. Doc held up the packed duffel. "Supplies, ammo and your antibiotics. I swept it for bugs. Clear. You're good to go."

"Thanks." They searched the premises for any identifying items and eliminated the fingerprints.

Hunter took one last look. "So much for this place being safe." He kneaded the muscles at the base of his neck.

"Doc, my plan is completely screwed. I was supposed to meet someone to have their new identification finalized today. Pictures, fingerprints, birth certificates, the works. No way that's happening. I have to find an alternative source."

"Then you know who to call." Doc tugged out a phone. "One of Logan's specials. For emergencies."

Hunter grabbed the secure equipment and dialed a number.

"Carmichael."

"Should I call you *Your Highness?*" Hunter said.

"Shove it, Graham," Logan grumbled. "My life is a pain in the butt tonight. I have to attend a meet-and-greet with a bunch of muckety-mucks from France and Germany in a few minutes. Luckily, Kat promised to make it worth my while later if I behave," he said. "I plan on smiling until my cheeks hurt tonight so she'll misbehave later. Now, what do you want so I can get on with the torture of my evening?"

Hunter had to smile. Despite the frustration, he could hear the contentment in his friend's voice. The man was so in love with Kat and his kids he couldn't see straight.

"Logan, I need help. I set up a rendezvous with your Texas contact. I missed the deadline and the contact number is no longer valid."

"Yeah, that's pretty standard." Logan paused and mumbled something to someone on his end. A few seconds later a door shut. "What aren't you telling me? You should have the resources to do this job in less time than I can find another option."

Hunter hated what he had to admit, but now was not the time to hold back from those he trusted. "I didn't give you all the information, Logan. I'm sorry, but this entire operation is unsanctioned. It's personal."

Logan didn't respond, but Hunter knew his friend was still on the other end.

"I have a son," Hunter said. "He's one, and his mother is in big danger. She's been mentioned in chatter."

Logan let out a low whistle, and Hunter knew the ex-CIA operative understood the implications.

"She and my son have to have new identities, but I need someone below the radar. Way far off so that no one could ever connect me to them."

He could hear Logan's fingers drumming on the table. "I may have an option. Where are you right now?"

"Florida Panhandle, but I need to get to Carder. I have to see that lawyer you recommended."

"Then this will work. Noah Bradford has a contact from when we worked a drug cartel job just across the border. She's a bit of a hermit, but the gal can get you anything you need. She's another Carder, Texas, connection and doesn't live too far from what used to be my ranch."

"Oh, man, I'm sorry about the Triple C."

"I made it out with my kids and Kat," Logan said. "That's all I care about."

"I may need more than one day in Carder to get everything done. Is there someplace out of the way where no one would think to look?"

"The ranch burned to the ground, but I have a small cabin near the back acre, not too far from a stream. The cowhands stayed there to guard the herd from rustlers back in the day. It's not much, but it's a roof."

Hunter let out a slow breath, one he'd been holding. At least his small family would have a place to sleep. "Thanks, Logan. I owe you."

"You helped me save Kat's life. You owe me nothing." Logan paused. "Just keep your son safe. In the end, family is all we have to hold on to."

Hunter ended the call and met Doc's gaze. "All I have to do is find a completely anonymous and unexpected way to get to Carder, Texas, without getting killed between here and there."

Chapter Seven

The rhythmic sound of the sea pulsing into the pier was the only sound. The desolate marina was eerily quiet. Darkness hung over the deserted area.

At Doc's signal, Hunter pressed Erin next to a foreclosed office building. "Don't come out until I motion to you."

She nodded. She'd been quiet. Too quiet. Hunter understood.

She'd still been upset with him when they'd returned the airboats.

Then Hunter had seen the blood.

He'd tried to protect Erin, but she'd walked right into a huge pool just outside the small outdoor stand.

The poor guy who'd sold them the boat had been facedown with his brains splattered around him.

Erin hadn't been able to look away. She had hardly said a word since.

The news indicated the man's death to be a suicide. Too much debt, a wife who left him.

Hunter knew better.

So did Erin.

His entire body tense, he scanned the area, then the water.

No movement except the occasional wave.

"You're sure they'll be here?" he asked Doc. "I'm not certain I'd want to touch this mission with a two-hundred-foot crane."

"They'll be here," Doc said.

"I don't get it," Hunter said. "What's their story?"

"Marty's husband died on 9/11. He was a firefighter. A real hero. He took a second trip up in the towers. He didn't make it out." Doc lifted his night-vision goggles and surveyed the horizon. "She and her husband's uncle are on a mission now. They've never let me down."

The hum of an engine pierced over the lapping of the water against the pier. They both ducked down. Doc swung his goggles toward the sound.

He didn't speak for a moment. Hunter's entire body crouched low, ready to take off.

"It's them." Doc smiled. "What did I tell you? Right on time."

A fishing boat rumbled toward the pier. The paint job had seen much better days. By the time it reached them, Hunter took a step back. "That is some boat. But seriously, Doc. Is it seaworthy? I need to get to Texas quickly. How fast can it possibly go?"

"Faster than you'd expect. I wouldn't judge this book by its cover. Besides, do you have a choice?" Doc whispered, "You can't risk the airport or the bus station."

"I know. They'll be watching for that, and I can't risk going cross-country. Even if we stay off the interstate, we could get caught on the wrong camera. I like it. No one will think to follow us on the water."

The boat settled beside the dock.

Hunter eyed the solid woman with a hat tilted on wild red hair. She stood on the bow. She also clearly ran things. The old guy at her side secured the boat and they strode over to Doc.

"So, what's so urgent I left a week's worth of fish swimming in the gulf?" She settled her arms on her hips and cocked her head.

"Hunter, this is Marty Zaring, Captain of *Precious Memories*. She'll get you near Corpus Christi."

"He a good guy?" she asked Doc.

"And when have I ever not hooked you up with a good guy?" Doc asked.

Marty winked and held out her hand to Hunter. "Fair enough. So you need passage on the down-low? Just you?"

Hunter motioned to Erin, and she emerged from the shadows, holding Brandon in her arms. "All three of us."

Marty stared at the baby and her expression softened. "He's a cute one, all right."

The grizzled man at her side walked over. "Ain't he the big boy?" The man's twinkle transformed his gruffer appearance. The guy could have been Santa Claus.

Erin's eyes widened, but Brandon reached out to the old guy and grinned.

"Crisp here loves kids. He can help take care of your son," Marty said.

"His parents need help," Crisp muttered. "They look like hell." He lifted Brandon above his head and he chuckled. "Get on the boat, you two. I'll take care of the young'n."

"I haven't given permission, Unc," Marty groused.

"Well...*Captain*...you actually gonna turn these three down?"

"No," the woman grumbled. "Get on board."

Doc leaned over to Hunter. "Have I ever steered you wrong?"

Hunter shook Doc's hand. "If you ever need anything—"

"I'll come looking. You owe me. Again," Doc said.

"Keep that family safe. And, Hunter…think twice about letting them go. You may regret it."

Doc turned to Erin and gave her a hug. "Take care of him. He won't take care of himself. Clean his back and make sure he takes the antibiotics I gave him."

"I'm right here," Hunter pointed out.

"And you suck at following orders, my friend." He saluted Marty and disappeared into the night.

Marty stepped forward and planted her hands on her hips. "Now that Doc's escaped, I have a few ground rules. This is my boat. I make the rules." She looked Hunter up and down. "I have to agree with Unc. You both look like hell. I have one extra cabin below, right past the galley. Get some rest, please. I don't want to have to chuck a dead body over the side. Coast Guard frowns on that sort of thing. Besides, I want you two out of sight most of the trip. There may not be quite as many cameras in the gulf as on land, but there are a few, and I already recognize the doctor from the television."

Hunter picked up the duffel and took one last look around. Nothing unusual, still deserted. Maybe they'd caught a break.

"You have weapons?" Marty asked.

"A submachine gun."

"Just keep them out of my way, but if we run into trouble, there's a cabinet in the galley with a padlock. You'll find what you need in there."

Hunter followed Erin over to Brandon. She held out her arms, but their son was fascinated with Crisp. He juggled Brandon and chuckled when the boy tugged at his beard. "Oh, yeah, I'm gonna make a sailor out of you, just like I did my nephew's wife. But *you* won't take over, will you, boy?" The sailor lifted Brandon over his head. "Whew! You're ripe, kiddo. Diaper change for you."

Without asking, he plucked Erin's makeshift diaper bag stuffed in the pocket on the side of the duffel. She and Hunter followed. Within seconds, the old seaman whisked one diaper aside and replaced it with another.

Hunter met Erin's gaze. "Faster than you, sweetheart."

"He knows what he's doing," Erin admitted.

Hunter nodded, wanting to follow his son and not let him out of sight. Crisp took the baby right outside the bridge.

"Captain's orders. You two go below. I'll keep him with me."

Erin shook her head. "I can't."

"Look, honey, I understand, but below it gets pretty rough. At least in the fresh air your son has less chance of being sick."

Erin looked over at Hunter, still uncertain.

A loud whistle sounded and a spotlight flashed on. It swept across the bay.

"Get down," Crisp said.

Hunter dragged Erin to the deck. With the light they could make out a large yacht. "Marty is right. We need to stay out of sight. Both of us."

"Good thinking, young man." Crisp smiled. "I'll watch your son. I give you my word. It's my bond."

Something in the man's eyes made Hunter nod. He ducked down beneath the deck and took Erin by the hand.

"Brandon will be okay?" she asked, biting her lip.

"I think so. Crisp can't take off with him—not that he would—and I don't want him to get sick."

She let out a small sigh and bobbed her head in agreement. They headed down the steps. The small galley was clean and pristine. Right past the tiny cooking area he pushed open the door.

A small bed took up the majority of space in the room.

Erin looked up at him. "They expect us to stay in here? I don't know if I can breathe."

Hunter took in Erin's pale face. "You can handle this. Just until we get out to sea."

The engine rumbled to life, and a loud horn sounded.

The boat swayed and lurched forward.

Erin teetered, then planted her feet. "This is crazy. How did we get here?"

He ran his knuckle along her cheek. "Life doesn't always work out like we plan. But we'll be okay. It'll work out."

"I know you're trying to calm me down, Hunter, but seriously. Given our luck the past few days, don't you think we should expect a hurricane?"

The boat lurched again, and Erin fell into Hunter in the small space. He caught her arms and looked down at her, his gaze hooded.

She knew that look. Knew it well. Her palms itched to tug Hunter closer and give in to the tension that had been rekindling between them. She knew it was dangerous to give in to her feelings.

Hunter might be determined to help them, but he didn't intend to make anything long-term. She wouldn't beg. She and Brandon had done just fine without Hunter. They would again.

No matter what kind of life they ended up with.

"I should rebandage your back," she said. "I promised Doc."

Hunter's gaze narrowed; then he seemed to back away. The spark nearly igniting the room diminished. "You're right," he said.

He slipped off his shirt and lay down on the bed.

Erin held her breath. Now that she wasn't concerned about him dying on her, she could take in the beauty of his shape. He really was perfection. The broad shoulders, the narrow waist, the defined muscles, his strength.

She reached into the duffel and pulled out the kit Doc had left.

"This might hurt."

"I trust you to be gentle," he said.

She didn't know how long it took her to remove and rebandage his injuries, but when she covered the last one, Erin swayed. She'd hurt him, and he hadn't made a sound.

She plopped on the bed.

Hunter lay on his side. "I didn't feel a thing," he whispered.

"Liar."

"Maybe," he acknowledged. "Wouldn't you rather I lie?"

She didn't have to consider. "No. I try to be honest. Lying just brings trouble." She settled on the bed and tucked her legs to her chin.

"Sometimes it keeps you alive," Hunter said.

"I can see how you'd think that, but I'm not very good at it. My mom could always tell when I lied."

She laid her cheek on her knees.

"You've never mentioned your parents before." Hunter stroked her arm with a finger. Erin shivered under his touch.

"Not exactly bedroom conversation. And I don't think we left that bed the whole week on Santorini."

"That's not true," Hunter protested. "We visited the beach."

"Yeah, your private beach. Nude. And we didn't stay vertical for long. Doesn't count."

"That was some week." Hunter tucked his arm beneath his ear. "Do you regret it?"

"How can I? I got Brandon." Erin toyed with the soft material of her T-shirt. "And I think I might very well be stuck in some terrorist's camp right now if we hadn't met. I understand what you did, Hunter, but next time, just tell me what's going on. Don't kidnap me again."

LEONA TAPPED HER FOOT on the floor of the secure infirmary. Antiseptic burned her nose and she waited.

The doctor exited through the door and swiped his badge.

"Well?" Leona said.

"I can't believe the guy is alive. He's going to need a lot of plastic surgery on his face and a prosthetic eye, but he's strong enough to talk to you."

Leona motioned to Trace. "Follow my lead."

He nodded his assent. She slipped her clearance into the reader and keyed in her code. With a deep breath, she walked inside.

The man lying in the bed had half his face swathed in bandages, an IV drip leading into his arm and straps securing him to the bed.

"Mr. Mahew, I presume."

He tried to shift against the restraints. Leona held out a folder. "You had a promising career. You qualified for Special Forces, surprisingly enough passed the psych exam, were an efficient assassin. And then you screwed up and earned yourself a dishonorable discharge. How does a man go from decorated hero to murderer? Hmmm?"

Terence toyed with the sheets. "Maybe I got fed up with the hypocrisy. Maybe I got tired of taking orders. Maybe I just like killing people and I got a better offer."

"I see. Money. It's what drives some people." Leona leaned over the bed. "But not you, does it, Mahew? We received some very interesting information from your hometown. When you were a teenager, a few too many farm animals went missing. Even a pet or two. No one could prove anything, but your mother—"

"Leave my mama out of this," Terence shouted.

Trace stepped in front of Leona and jammed his forearm against Terence's throat. "You raise your voice again, slimeball, and you'll wish I hadn't saved your life," he said.

Leona patted Trace's arm for show. The man should have been an actor. He backed away. "So, Terence, your mother doesn't have to know the details of your extracurricular activities. She seems like a God-fearing woman. But to keep your actions quiet, I need some leverage. I need to provide my boss with information."

Terence shook his head. "I don't know anything. I only talked to them on the phone. I don't know who he was. We never met."

"You'd recognize his voice?"

"Yeah. I guess. Had sort of a British accent with a bit of Arabic thrown in. All I know is that he wanted Dr. Jamison and her kid. He wanted them both alive."

"This isn't new information, Terence," Leona chastised. "You're going to need to do better if you want to get out of this facility alive." She leaned over him and walked her fingers from his breastbone to his neck. She pressed her thumb against one carotid artery, and her fingers on the second. "Think, Terence."

One eyelid blinked several times. The man grew paler as she increased the force against the vulnerable arteries. He understood exactly what she was doing.

With her other hand, Leona toyed with the area just below his ear. His vagus nerve. The right blow and she could stop his heart from beating.

"Okay, okay," Terence said. "Just let me breathe."

She released her grip and folded her arms in front of her. "I'm waiting."

Terence gulped in some air. "When I told my contact a guy with skills helped Dr. Jamison escape, my client didn't hesitate. He blurted out a name."

Leona leaned toward him. "What did he call the man?" she asked.

"Graham."

Oh, boy. The implications pierced Leona's gut. Graham's name was top secret. If the person who had hired Terence knew that name, then they had an insider.

It could be anyone.

Particularly someone new.

Leona whirled around to Trace. "Get out," she said, unable to keep the fury from her voice.

"Ma'am?"

"I said get out. Wait for me in my office, and don't talk to anyone."

Back stiff, Padgett walked out of the room, closing the door quietly.

Leona paced. She couldn't breathe. She had to think. Hunter and Erin were in even more danger than she'd realized. She had to pinpoint the threat.

"You said the caller had a Middle Eastern accent. I need you to think, Terence. Was the man you spoke with faking the accent?"

She'd tipped her hand, but she had to ask the question.

"If I tell you, will you get me out of here?"

"Maybe."

"Okay, lady. I'll play."

For several moments Terence just stared at her. Finally, he spoke.

"Here's the thing. If I had to bet, I'd say he was faking. His English was too good."

Leona turned on her heel and opened the door.

"Wait a minute. I want out."

"Maybe tomorrow," Leona said.

For now, she had a traitor to track down, and she had to make contact with Hunter. He'd cut her off, but he needed to know that he wasn't safe. Not anywhere.

If this was an inside job, then whoever wanted Erin Jamison had the means to find her, no matter where they hid.

THE BOAT ROCKED BENEATH THEM, and Hunter studied the profile of the woman who'd lain in his arms all night. She'd been through so much, and it wasn't over, not by a long shot. He'd give anything to make it better.

A loud bellowing horn sounded.

Erin stirred, then stretched, the material showcasing her lush curves.

Hunter swallowed. What he wouldn't give—

A loud shout catapulted Hunter to his feet.

Erin bolted up. "What was that?"

Thundering footsteps rushed down the stairs. Crisp threw open the door, his eyes frantic. Blood ran down his cheek.

"We're being boarded."

"Where's Brandon?" Erin shouted.

"My room," Crisp said.

Erin raced to the old man's room and scooped up Brandon.

"Get in the cabin," Hunter said. "Barricade the door and keep the gun trained on it. Don't let anyone in but me."

She nodded.

Hunter grabbed a submachine gun and a Bowie.

Gunfire spewed.

"Marty!" Crisp yelled.

Hunter led them up the stairs. He bolted onto the deck.

A man dressed in black had pinned Marty. "Where are the woman and the kid?"

Marty elbowed the guy in the chest. He whirled her around and slugged her across the cheek.

She went down.

Crisp bellowed and raised his weapon.

Before he could pull the trigger, though, Hunter took the shot. The guy dropped like a stone.

A grappling hook soared over the side of the boat. "There are more coming."

"Not if I can help it," Hunter said.

He raced to the rail and sprayed the two men rappelling up the side of the boat. They sank below the water.

Arms grabbed him from behind. Hunter twisted.

The guy countered his move.

What the hell?

Hunter slipped his leg between his attacker's.

Another counter.

The guy knew his moves, had the same training.

"Bet you don't know this one," Hunter grunted.

He pulled a variation on a high school wrestling move. The guy lost his balance. Hunter didn't need another opening. He slammed the heel of his hand against the guy's nose. Just that fast, it was over. The guerrilla hit the deck, unseeing, unmoving.

Hunter whirled around.

A siren sounded.

"*Precious Memories*. This is the Coast Guard. Prepare to be boarded."

A splash sounded on the side, then the roar of a Zodiac's outboard motor.

Crisp shouted and rushed over to a downed Marty, hidden behind a large crane. "You okay, honey?" He cupped his niece's cheek.

She blinked. "That wasn't fun," she groused.

Hunter bent over her. Marty's nose was broken, and her cheek bruised. "You're going to have quite the shiner. Nice move, though."

Marty clutched the fire truck pendant around her neck. "I had a good teacher."

A spotlight shone on the deck.

"Get below," Marty hissed. "I'll keep them busy. There's an escape raft tucked on the outside of the boat, starboard side, away from the Coast Guard cutter. They can't find you here."

Hunter clasped Marty's hand. "Thank you."

"Just keep your family safe, Hunter. No one deserves to lose theirs."

She kissed the pendant and then closed her eyes.

"Marty!"

Hunter placed his hands against her neck. She'd just passed out.

The old man's eyes glistened with tears. "I can't lose her, too."

"You won't. She's tougher than both of us."

The cutter attached itself to *Precious Memories*.

"Get out of here," Crisp said. "She'll wring my neck if you get caught."

"Show yourself," a voice bellowed over a megaphone.

Crisp stood, hands raised. "We need medical attention."

Hunter sneaked down the stairs to Erin. God bless her, she'd already packed everything. "Did I ever tell you you're one smart woman?" Hunter said.

He hauled the duffel over his shoulder and led Erin to the galley.

"Aren't we going on deck?" she asked.

"Not if we don't want to be interrogated." Hunter knelt below the table and pressed out. Sea air flowed in. He peered outside. Clear. The raft was right where Marty had described.

Within minutes, Hunter had the boat inflated. He bundled Erin and Brandon into the boat and tossed in their supplies.

He glanced at the shore. Thank goodness they were close. They paddled away from the boat and the flashing sirens.

"Where are we?" Erin whispered. She kept looking over her shoulder.

"South of Corpus Christi. Hopefully our ride will be here. We're not that far off schedule."

Hunter maneuvered the raft between boats. They'd made it. As covertly as possible, he hit the shore and crouched behind a building. Erin held Brandon.

Soon a sheriff's car pulled up across the way.

Hunter held out his hand. "Let's go."

"Cops?"

"Not just any cop. You're about to meet one of the few lawmen I can believe in. Blake Redmond. The sheriff from Carder, Texas."

A soft rumbling noise sounded from a pier not far away. Hunter squinted toward the sound. He waited and watched.

No movement.

No nothing.

A bad feeling skittered down his spine. He grabbed Brandon. "We're not staying here any longer. Let's go."

They ran to the sheriff's car.

Hunter dove into the backseat.

"Go! Go! Go!"

Chapter Eight

The sheriff's vehicle squealed away from the shoreline. Hunter ducked down and held Erin next to him.

When they'd cleared the majority of civilization, he raised his head.

"So, Hunter, wanna tell me what the hell you've gotten yourself into?" Blake asked.

"Not really."

"Good thing I trust Hunter or I'd kick you to the asphalt."

Blake turned on his lights and hit the accelerator. They made good time to Carder. Only about three o'clock.

They passed through both of the stoplights in Carder, Texas, and Blake pulled up outside a nondescript brick house Hunter had visited only a few months after Brandon had been born.

"Logan told me you had business with Exley," Blake said once the vehicle stopped. "If you want it done today, we're up against closing time. The old guy generally takes off around three."

Hunter could tell the sheriff didn't like not knowing what was going down in his town. Well, the local lawman would have to stay unhappy. "Thanks. We'll only be a minute."

Hunter turned in the seat. Brandon was asleep and hopefully would stay that way for a while. "I need you to come in with me, Erin."

She nodded.

"I'll keep an eye on him," Blake offered.

Erin slipped out of the backseat and took Hunter's hand. "What are we doing here?"

"I learned about Brandon soon after he was born," Hunter said.

She stopped in the middle of the sidewalk and stared at him. "How?"

"Do we have to discuss this now?"

She planted her hands on her hips. "I'm not walking into that office without an explanation."

"I missed you," Hunter said, trying to figure out how he could possibly explain leaving her alone to give birth to and raise their son by herself. "I came back and saw you when you were about seven months pregnant. I started keeping track, making sure you were okay."

Erin shook her head and stared at him. "My God, do you know how frightened I was, how terrified? I was all alone in the world, with a baby and no family, and you were just watching?" She paced back and forth. "Why?"

"Because I knew that if I tried to be with you, I could get you killed," Hunter said through clenched teeth. "You think I didn't want to be there?" He gripped her arm. "I wanted you, Erin. I still want you, but in my profession I've made enemies. Powerful enemies. If they ever connect us, they could use you and Brandon to get to me. I couldn't take that chance."

He might have been able to take anger, but the hurt expression in her eyes gutted him to the core. "So you knew about us. Why are we here?"

"I wanted to make certain if something happened to me, you and Brandon were taken care of. I set up a trust for our son. Now, since you will have a new identity, I need to give you everything."

Erin rubbed her eyes with her hands. "Fine," she said, her tone devoid of emotion. "Let's just get it done."

He rubbed at the tension in his neck, working its way up into his scalp. A supersized headache threatened, but at least she hadn't refused his gift. He'd wondered if she might. He'd expected her to. Had she finally come to accept the reality of the situation? Hunter studied her set jaw. He couldn't read her reaction, and that worried him.

With a sigh, he pushed open the door to the lawyer's office and stepped inside.

A horrible smell overcame him. One he recognized all too well.

Erin slapped her hand over her mouth and backed away. "Oh, my God, what is that?"

Hunter palmed his weapon from the small of his back then pushed Erin out the door. "Go get the sheriff." He paused. "Erin? Do you still have the gun I gave you?"

She nodded.

"Get it out. And stay with Brandon."

Her features pale, but determined, Erin raced to the car while Hunter scanned the receptionist's area. The room was immaculate—and empty.

Nothing seemed out of place except for the absolute quiet, and the scent of a decaying body.

Any other time, Hunter might have called out, but the current situation was anything but normal. His internal radar had gone into overdrive.

Footsteps thundered behind Hunter. Sheriff Blake Redmond let out a loud curse. He clicked his radio. "I need backup at Exley's. And get the coroner's office over here."

Blake sidled up to Hunter. "This is a crime scene. What do you think you're still doing in here?"

"Look, Sheriff, you don't know me, but I need to do a quick search."

Blake grabbed Hunter's collar. Hunter let him. "Why should I? Why shouldn't I take you in for questioning since you wanted to see Exley, and now somebody in his office is dead?"

Hunter met the sheriff's gaze. "Look, Logan trusts you, and I'm asking for your help. If you care anything about saving those innocent lives sitting in your car, I need to know why Exley died."

Blake stared Hunter down. "You have five minutes. And you're not leaving my sight."

"Deal," Hunter said.

He crossed over to the door leading into Exley's office. Blake handed him a pair of gloves. Hunter slipped them on, turned the knob and pushed inside.

The scent wasn't as bad as some of the killing fields from the worst assignments overseas, but he choked on the odor just the same.

A woman's legs stuck out from behind the desk.

"Oh, man, it's Mrs. Exley. She was her husband's receptionist. Didn't trust all the pretty young things, she used to say," Blake commented.

Hunter rounded the desk. The woman's neck had been snapped. Even summer decomposition didn't hide the angle of her head. And Hunter knew exactly the move the perp had used.

Damn it.

Now that he was behind the desk, he saw the white-haired lawyer's body. It was hard to tell given the state of the body, but blood caked the side of the poor guy's head.

"Look at the corner of the desk," Hunter pointed out.

Blake looked around the room. "Nothing much has been touched except this drawer."

Something sank in the pit of Hunter's belly. When he'd visited Exley to sign Brandon's trust paperwork, the man had pulled Hunter's file from that location.

He peered into the open drawer. A file labeled *Clay Griffin* sat empty, except for a small piece of paper inside.

Before Blake could stop him, Hunter snagged the sheet.

Hunter Graham.

He let out a solid curse.

"What is it?" Blake asked, and looked at the slip in Hunter's hand. "Damn it. You're messing with evidence."

"This won't help you, Sheriff. You won't find the murderer." He pocketed the slip of paper.

Blake's jaw throbbed. "You know who did it."

Hunter stared at the man and his wife who had never done anything to anyone. By asking Exley for help, he'd effectively signed the couple's death warrant.

If Hunter had held out any hope that he might find a way to be with Erin and Brandon, that flicker had been put on ice.

Whoever had done this had known exactly who they were looking for. Otherwise the room would have been in shambles. No, they knew the name Clay Griffin. Now they had not only connected Clay Griffin to Hunter Graham, but they had also connected him to Erin and Brandon Jamison. There were a dozen terrorist organizations that wanted Hunter dead. And now they had the leverage they wanted.

Everything General Miller had warned Hunter about had come true.

His boss had been right. He couldn't afford a family. Not now. Not ever.

"Don't just stand there. Who killed them?"

"I don't know, Sheriff." Another truth. "What I do

know is that all my plans to protect those two in your car
have been blown all to hell."

ERIN COULDN'T BELIEVE THE subterfuge that Hunter had
engineered. They'd driven to a nearby town and back,
switched cars twice and now she and Brandon sat in the
backseat of a gray SUV that seemed to disappear against
the dusky sky.

Brandon had fallen asleep and after the past few days
he was probably out for the night. Thank goodness.

Hunter's entire body had been on high alert since he'd
come out of the lawyer's office. She still couldn't believe
the poor man and his wife had been murdered, but the cold
look in Hunter's eyes terrified her.

He turned onto a dirt road, and they bounced across
the landscape.

"Where are we going now?" she asked, unable to keep
the fatigue from her voice.

"Someplace safe, I hope. At least until I can arrange to
get you permanently away from here."

Erin leaned her head back against the seat. "These plans
of yours get more and more complicated, Hunter. Why
can't we just stop? Surely the government agency you work
for can help us?"

Before Hunter could respond, he slammed on the
brakes. A black SUV sat in front of a small cabin.

"Who's there?"

"I don't know."

Hunter shifted into Reverse until Sheriff Redmond
stepped from the cabin. The tall man held up his hand in
greeting. Hunter let out a slow curse and pulled the car
forward, parking it.

Erin exited the vehicle and reached into the backseat for

a sleeping Brandon. She unhitched the carrier that snapped on the frame. At least Brandon was secure.

Hunter grabbed the duffel from the back end. "I didn't expect to see you here, Sheriff."

A small boy peered out from behind him, and the sheriff ruffled the boy's head. "This is Ethan."

A woman appeared beside Blake. A very pregnant woman. "And I'm Amanda Redmond." She smiled at Erin. "When Blake told me you were staying out here, I thought you could use a few feminine touches. Not to mention baby proofing the place."

Erin held the carrier handle. Ethan ran over and looked inside. "He's little. What's his name?"

"Brandon."

"I'm getting a baby sister soon," Ethan said proudly. "I'm going to be the best big brother ever."

"I'm sure you will be. She's a lucky little girl."

Ethan grinned. "Do you wanna see what my mommy brought? She made her extraspecial macaroni and cheese *and* cookies. We even brought stuff for s'mores."

The boy held out his hand to Erin and she followed him inside the cabin. It was small, just two rooms, but she could see that Amanda had stocked up. A tin of cookies sat on the table. A box of food and fresh fruits and vegetables were in the refrigerator. Erin set Brandon's carrier in the corner out of the way.

She looked around, and her eyes burned at the care a complete stranger had taken. She turned to the auburn-haired woman, whose hand was tucked into her husband's.

"Thank you so much. You can't know—"

Amanda reached out and patted Erin's arm. "You'd be surprised how much I understand. Blake and I don't know exactly what's going on, but it wasn't long ago that I didn't know where I could turn to. This town became my haven. I hope it can become yours."

Erin sent Hunter a sidelong glance. If she had to leave her world behind, a place like Carder would have been nice.

He gave her a small shake of his head, and she sighed. Not that his reaction surprised her. While she hadn't developed friendships in Pensacola because of her work schedule, she'd hoped that someday she would be a part of a neighborhood where anyone could knock on her door asking for a cup of sugar or some hot chocolate and marshmallows and be welcome.

Now she wondered if even that small slice of life would be forbidden. Would she always be looking over her shoulder, searching the crowd for danger, being suspicious of every new person to come into her life?

For a split second she'd even wondered if Blake and Amanda Redmond could have ulterior motives. How did Hunter live this way?

She hated it.

Unfortunately, she'd also accepted that this would be her life.

"What does the Triple C look like?" Hunter asked Blake.

The sheriff let out a low whistle. "Burned to the ground. They razed the place and built a barn for the horse, but it's gonna take time to rebuild. All that's left is the surveillance equipment. Not that it helped much."

Erin's ears perked up. "Does it work?"

"Logan said he planned to replace it."

"Do you think he'd care if I took a look? I might find something I can use." She didn't know how much money she'd have. She'd bet Logan had top-notch equipment Maybe she could put together a security system so she could sleep at night.

"Have at it," Blake said. "I'm not even sure Logan will come back."

Amanda cleared her throat. Ethan had leaned against Amanda, and his eyelids had gone heavy.

"We'd better head out," Blake said. "Someone's ready for bed."

Amanda gave Erin a hug. "If you need anything, call me," she whispered. "I learned the hard way that not asking for help when you need it causes much more trouble than staying silent."

Hunter reached out his hand to Blake. "Thank you. We won't be here long, but we appreciate the hospitality."

"Anyone Logan trusts is okay by me," Blake said. "His word means a lot in these parts."

The Redmonds pulled away from the cabin, the dust stirring up. A red sunset burned over the horizon.

Erin leaned against the doorjamb and closed her eyes. "I don't know if I can stay awake long enough for dinner," she said. "Do you think there's a bathtub in this place? I would love a hot soak."

Hunter opened the bathroom door. "You're in luck. A claw-foot tub. Someone set this place up for more than a couple of hunters."

"Hop in. I'll heat up dinner."

After grabbing a nightshirt from the duffel, Erin searched under the sink. She rooted around and found some bath salts. Heaven.

Hot water poured from the faucet and she sprinkled the lavender crystals into the water. One dip of her toe, then her foot, and Erin sank down into the steaming heat.

She let out a long sigh, closed her eyes and faded beneath the water. For a few brief moments, she allowed the heat to melt the tension from her muscles. The sounds of the refrigerator and cabinet doors opening and closing filtered from outside.

She'd had more than one fantasy of Hunter joining her in a tub, candles burning all around and their entwined bodies sloshing water all over the floor. Just like in the movies.

Somewhere inside her, she hadn't given up on that dream. But each time hope reignited in her heart, something beyond her control doused it.

She'd learned the day her parents died that life wasn't fair. Why did she keep trying? Even her research attempted to circumvent Mother Nature. Was she a fool for trying to change anything?

"Have you turned into a prune yet?" Hunter called out.

A delighted giggle made her smile. Brandon was up. At least for the moment. As quick as she could, Erin dressed and exited the bathroom.

"Was it as good as you hoped?" he asked, setting a casserole dish on the table.

"Better."

Hunter doled out a plate and handed Erin a serving. Then he put a smaller amount in a small plastic bowl. Amanda had even brought a baby spoon.

"Do you think half got into his stomach?" Hunter laughed after he'd tried to feed Brandon. "Because the other half is definitely either on his face or the floor."

"I said mac and cheese was his favorite. Not that he necessarily ate it all." Erin took another bite. She didn't know what kind of cheese Amanda had used, but whatever it was made Erin's mouth water. "I have to get this recipe," she said.

"Well, I have to admit, Amanda Redmond makes my mom's mac and cheese look pedestrian." Hunter pushed his chair back from the table to keep Brandon from further wreaking havoc on their dinner.

"What kind did your mom make?"

"From a box. If we had the money to buy it."

"What about your dad?"

Hunter looked down at Brandon with a heartbreaking expression. "I never knew him. Some guy my mom dated in high school. He left when she found out she was pregnant." He looked up and met Erin's gaze. "I promised myself I'd never do something like that. My own choices kept me from keeping that vow. I'm sorry."

"Does your mom know about your job?" Erin asked.

"She died when I was sixteen. Too much work, not enough food or health care."

"What did you do?"

Hunter shrugged. "Hung out on the streets until I turned eighteen. There was an army recruiting office across from one of the shelters. I got my G.E.D. and signed up. At least it was a steady paycheck. I found out I was good at it. The guys became my family. They had my back."

"Like Logan. And Doc."

"And General Miller. He hand-selected me. No one made me feel like I was really worth something until he did. He taught me I could do anything."

"My parents gave me that gift before they died."

With a look that bored into her soul, Hunter captured her gaze. "We've both lost. We've both overcome. I hadn't realized." Hunter rose and Brandon snuggled into his chest. "I assumed we were so different. From the moment we met on Santorini I wanted you, but I also recognized you were from a different stratosphere than me."

Openmouthed, Erin couldn't comprehend his words. "When you walked up to me, I thought *you'd* made the mistake."

Hunter stepped toward her and cupped her cheek. "I didn't make a mistake, Erin. You brought light into my life like I'd never known."

Brandon's heavy eyelids blinked again and again, then closed, despite just waking up. Her son was clearly exhausted.

"Let me get him ready for bed."

While Hunter washed the dishes, she slipped Brandon into his pajamas and settled him into the playpen that Amanda had brought. Soon enough, their son was snoring away.

She bent over the side and pushed a lock of black hair from his forehead. "Good night, cutie. Mommy loves you."

She stood, and a warm heat caressed her back. Hunter's hands rested on her shoulders. He turned her into his arms and stared down at her.

"I probably shouldn't kiss you," he said. "We both know nothing can come of it."

His eyes seduced her like molten chocolate, and she was so very tempted. She lifted her fingers to his lips. They parted under her touch. "You hurt me," she said. "You shredded my heart when you left me alone. If I give in to these feelings, what will be left of me?"

He clasped her hand in his. "I can't answer that. All I can tell you is I've been wanting to hold you since I left you in Santorini. Will you let me, Erin? Will you let me love you even though you know we'll have to say goodbye?"

His hands rubbed her shoulders, and all of the scientific logic Erin had counted on all her life left her. For the first time since that island paradise, she let her heart rule her head.

She wrapped her arms around Hunter's neck and pulled him down to her. "Love me, Hunter. I'm tired of denying what I feel. Until we have to say goodbye, love me."

LEONA WALKED INTO TRACE Padgett's office and threw down the latest watch list on his desk. "What's the meaning of this?" She stabbed her finger at Hunter's name. "A risk to national security? Suspect mental state. Who ordered this?"

"Ma'am—"

The patronization in his voice annoyed her to no end. "Don't *ma'am* me, Trace. Explain yourself."

"Terence Mahew remembered something else, ma'am. He said the man who contacted him said something about knowing Erin Jamison. I discovered Clay Griffin and Erin Jamison had an affair more than a year ago. Someone within this office tried to cover up the relationship."

Leona closed her eyes. The jig was up. She'd hoped she'd plugged all the holes. Clearly she'd failed.

"So he slept with her. So what?"

She had to find out how much Padgett knew. And how much Kent knew.

"Hunter Graham has a lot of contacts. Erin Jamison began development of her prototype several years ago." Trace pulled out his notebook. "Graham has made several trips to Florida over the past fourteen months. I think he's been working on a payoff since he met her. If we don't find him, Erin Jamison could end up dead, and her prototype in terrorists' hands."

Leona stood and tapped her finger to her forehead. Trace Padgett was very, very good. Too good.

"Where do you think Graham has gone?"

"The chatter is quiet. If I were Hunter, I wouldn't stay in Florida. If I were going to do a meet, I'd go to Mexico. On the border of New Mexico or Arizona probably."

"See what you can find out from border patrol. See if there's any unusual activity.

Not bad, Trace. Not bad at all.

Leona left the room, her hands quivering.

This was not good.

Hunter was ignoring her calls. She had no idea where he was. The plans had gone to hell.

She picked up her secure phone and dialed a number. "We have a problem. Are the offshore accounts secure?"

"Of course," her husband said. "I'm ready when you're ready, my love."

"If Hunter doesn't call soon, we may be screwed."

"He'll call, Leona. He trusts you."

"I hope so. Once he calls, we have to move fast. We have to end Hunter Graham once and for all."

Chapter Nine

Hunter couldn't believe the words coming from Erin's lips.

"Love me," she whispered.

How could he resist?

He folded his arms around her and took possession of her mouth in a way that had haunted his dreams for far too long.

She whimpered against his lips and he pulled back. "Did I hurt you?"

Her eyes shone with unshed tears. "Don't stop. I've waited forever to feel this way again."

"So have I, sweetheart, so have I."

Unwilling to release her, Hunter walked her into the small bedroom. He closed them in and flipped on a small bedside lamp. The log walls were enveloped in a soft light, bathing her hair so it glimmered like strands of sunlight.

He thrust his fingers into the softness and captured her gaze. "Last chance, but please don't ask me not to make love to you."

"Make me forget, Hunter. Make me forget everything but you. At least for tonight."

Hunter backed them against the edge of the bed and fell back, Erin sprawled on top of him. "Take what you want," he murmured. "I'm all yours."

She grinned and straddled his hips. He could feel her

heat beneath the thin nightshirt. She squirmed on top of him, and his body surged into hardness.

"You want me," Erin said. She bent over him, and the soft curves of her breasts pressed into his chest.

Hunter couldn't wait to see her any longer. He lifted the long T-shirt over her head. He cupped her weight in his hand and kissed the soft arc, working his way down. His tongue flicked her hardened nipple, and Erin let out a small gasp.

Her hips ground against him. "Don't make me wait. Not this time."

He flipped her beneath him and nuzzled her neck. His jeans-covered leg slid between hers and he pressed against her.

She let out a soft groan and arched up. He'd forgotten how giving, how passionate, how open she was to his touch. "You are truly beautiful."

"And you are too dressed," Erin said softly. She flicked open one button, then the next and the next, easing his shirt off his shoulders. Hunter shrugged out of the garment. Erin's fingers went to the button of his jeans. She scraped a knuckle down his zipper.

He couldn't stop the low groan. "Don't, or this will be over before we start."

She stilled and within seconds, Hunter had shucked his pants. He settled between her thighs, his entire body hard; then he groaned.

"Condom," he moaned.

"Please, tell me you have one."

He shook his head. "I haven't been with anyone since…" He glanced away. He hadn't wanted anyone, not after Erin. He'd gone out with a couple of women, trying to forget, but those emerald eyes would not leave his memory.

Her eyes widened and she let her head fall back. "Me, either."

Hunter moved to the side. "I won't be careless with you again, Erin. If things were different..."

He didn't finish the words. He'd love to have a family with Erin, to be with her always. He breathed in deeply, trying desperately to calm himself.

"What about the nightstand?" she whispered.

"You don't think..."

He reached for the drawer and pulled out a brand-new box. The sight brought his body back to life. He grabbed a packet and rolled onto his back. "Will you?"

"My pleasure."

She used Hunter's body as her own personal playground, exploring each and every inch of skin. Nipping him with her teeth, letting her fingernails drag down his chest until he groaned with anticipation, she teased him more and more.

By the time she'd prepared him, Hunter writhed with want.

"That's it. I have to have you," he growled. In one fluid motion he sank inside her, and she gripped him, holding him close.

How long had he waited to feel this way again?

She wrapped her legs around him. Hunter's heart thudded against his chest. She moved with him as if they'd never been apart.

The world fell away. There was only her, only him, only them.

Faster, harder, stronger, longer.

His body stretched tight, he plunged in one last time and shuddered. Her body quivered in response and she let out a long, slow sigh.

"Better than I remember," she whispered. "Perfect."

He tossed the condom in the trash and spooned her against his body, wrapping her safe and warm. She leaned her head back against him. "Thank you."

He threaded their fingers together and held her close, his eyelids growing heavy. Her breathing evened out, but she didn't move, didn't pull away from him, she simply buried her hips closer and settled into a sound sleep.

Hunter sighed with contentment. He never wanted to move again. For tonight, for this moment, Erin belonged to him. They belonged together.

TERENCE COULDN'T FEEL HIS FACE. He rested his hand on the bandage. Perhaps that was for the best. He'd tried calling his mother. She hadn't answered.

He had to get out of this place.

The weakness had dissipated, though he hadn't let his jailers know. He'd had the training, he knew their games, their strategies. He just didn't know what they really wanted. He'd received mixed signals.

The guy who'd brought him here would have been happy to kill him at any moment. The woman, too.

And yet they hadn't.

If they'd wanted to get rid of him, all they'd have to do was hand him over to his clients. Terence had no doubt his mother wouldn't have enough parts left to cremate.

Heavy footsteps sounded down the hall and headed his way. The steel door opened. The man entering held power. He was confident. Terence scooted up in bed. He had a bad feeling.

"Mr. Mahew, the worst our military has to offer."

Terence scowled.

"Oh, you take offense? Too damn bad." The man leaned over his bed. "I want to know everything you know, and I want to know now. This is your last chance."

Terence shivered slightly. Something in the man's cadence, something in his words didn't sit right. He shifted away from the narrowed stare.

"Who hired you, Terence?"

"I told you, I don't know. It was a cash job. Should have been easy money."

"You knew Graham's name."

"I'd never seen him before that day. Some idiot let his name slip on the phone afterward. That's all, I swear it."

"That's what I expected you'd say."

The man tugged out a syringe. "This will stop your heart. The doctors will think the injuries were just too much for you. Your mother will have a body to bury, and, Terence...perhaps this deal that you agreed to wasn't the most profitable." The man's voice had dropped into a very familiar accent.

"Oh, my God. It's you? What are you doing here?"

"Haven't figured it out yet? No one from overseas hired you, fool. You were chosen for a reason, Terence. You are expendable."

The needle plunged into Terence's arm. He looked down to see the syringe sticking out. Liquid heat burned under his skin.

He hadn't expected this. He could usually smell a setup before the guy opened his mouth. He'd gotten greedy.

"You've figured it out, haven't you, Terence? You were never going to get out of this job alive. I needed a fall guy. You're that man."

A strange heat pulsed under Terence's skin. He blinked. His pulse raced. His throat closed off.

Terence clawed at his throat. "Please...won't...tell."

A door slammed open.

"No one has authority to be in...here."

Terence turned to the woman. He reached out a hand. "Help...me."

Her eyes widened. "Oh, no. It can't be you. Tell me this isn't true."

"Damn it, Leona. Why did you have to be so damned efficient?"

Terence blinked again. His vision blurred. The man covered the woman's mouth with his hand and plunged something into her arm.

He's killed you, too.

Terence heard the words in his head, but nothing escaped his lips.

His breathing turned shallow. Darkness faded in.

Mama. I wanted you to have a nice house. I tried, Mama. I really tried.

THE TURQUOISE SEA LAPPED against the vacation bungalow. Hunter lay in bed, Erin cuddled against him, and he watched her sleep.

He toyed with the silky blond tresses, letting them slip through his fingers. He couldn't get over how beautiful she was.

They'd had six days together. Six passionate, unbelievable days, and he knew it was only a matter of time until he had to leave.

"You're watching me again, Clay," she whispered, her eyes still closed.

He winced. Just once, he wanted her to use his real name, but like so many wishes in his life, he couldn't hope that his dreams would come true.

He kissed her shoulder, tasting the smooth skin, then nipping her with his teeth. A shiver skittered through her. He loved her responsiveness.

She turned in his arms, and the sheet fell away from her

breasts, revealing the soft curves. After their first night together, she didn't hide herself from him. She trusted him.

She shouldn't, but how could he warn her and not ruin everything?

He cupped her cheek, and his body hardened as she pressed closer to him. Her husky laughter made him smile. Naked thighs tangled with his; an arching of her hips elicited an unrestrained groan. It started in his belly and rumbled in his chest.

Erin smiled at him, welcoming, passionate, loving.

She leaned over and kissed him, her lips doing things to his mouth that he'd never experienced.

"I'm oh so lucky," she said. "I came to celebrate being buried in a lab for the past six years, and I found you." She cuddled into him and nearly purred.

Hunter's body leaped at her touch, even as his heart twisted in regret.

Maybe, just maybe, he could keep the world away from them for a while longer. He rolled her to her back and settled between her thighs, his body pressing against hers.

"I'm the lucky one," he said as he buried himself into her.

She closed her eyes and let out a groan of passion. She hid nothing from him. He reveled in her honesty.

"I never thought anyone like you would love me," he whispered, the truth in those words wrenched from his soul.

He moved against her. She wrapped her legs around his waist, and together they escaped the world in each other's arms. He lost himself, captured by her heart and her love. He wanted her. Always. Forever.

The vibrating phone in his pants filtered across the room.

No. It couldn't be happening. Not now.

But he knew.

His dream was over.

Reality had come calling.

And he would have to say goodbye.

MORNING LIGHT STREAMED THROUGH the shutters. Erin stretched, her body sore in unexpected and wonderful places.

Then she remembered.

The past, the present, the unknown future.

She crossed her arms over her bare breasts and searched the edge of the bed for her nightshirt. She slipped into it and peeked out the bedroom door.

Hunter sat in a rocking chair, Brandon in his arms, staring out the front window. A cup of coffee rested on the table at Hunter's side. He didn't look happy or satisfied.

She cleared her throat. He turned to her, his gaze warming, but cautious at the same time. Something had happened. "What's wrong?"

"Logan called. We're set to meet with the woman who will provide you and Brandon with your new identification papers."

So it was over already. Erin closed her eyes, the feeling of loss indescribable. When he'd left before, she'd been in shock. This time she'd known it was coming, but it didn't hurt any less. "When?"

"This afternoon."

He looked outside. "Do you ride?"

"Not for a long time. Why?"

"Do you want to? Logan has a couple of horses he keeps on hand in a barn not too far from here."

"It's safe?" she asked.

"Safer than sitting in one place any longer," Hunter said.

His words sent a chill through her. She rubbed her hands

over her arms, trying to ease the foreboding. It did no good. "Then let's go. I'm getting claustrophobic anyway."

It would do them both good to get away from these four cloying walls.

Half an hour later, Hunter drove the SUV over a series of dirt roads to a newly constructed barn.

Erin exited the vehicle and looked at the utter destruction of the surrounding area. The earth had been scorched. Half a dozen buildings had burned to the ground. There was nothing left. "What happened here? It looks like a war zone."

"This was the Triple C Ranch. Logan's ancestral home. It used to be a fortress, until he crossed some demented, determined people who liked guerrilla tactics and to play with explosives. This is the result."

"And we're safe here?"

"We're never safe, Erin, but no one lives here. Construction crews are just starting to rebuild the ranch and the main house, and the ranch hands still take care of the horses. Logan is now Prince Consort of Bellevaux, and he and his wife and kids live there."

Erin's eyes widened. "Logan's wife is that queen in Europe they just discovered?"

"The same."

Hunter entered the barn and saddled a gentle-looking mare. Erin looked down and strapped Brandon more closely in his baby harness. His weight was reassuring on her chest.

"You sure you don't want me to take him?" Hunter asked. "He's kind of heavy."

Erin shook her head. "I need to hold him right now. I'm feeling a little shaky."

Hunter's face clouded, but he nodded and saddled a large black stallion. "Let's head out."

The mare walked slowly, but it still took a few minutes for Erin to get comfortable. Finally, she relaxed into the horse's rhythm.

"You've got a good seat," Hunter said.

She glanced at him. "I learned when I was a kid. I guess you don't forget."

They rode past the destroyed structures and picked up a faint trail that wound around and led into some rolling hills nearby.

Erin glanced up at a telephone pole. The sophisticated security monitoring system was attached to the top of the pole. With equipment like that, it was amazing anyone got near the ranch. How much was functional?

She said nothing until they passed a second one that had fallen onto the ground.

"Wait," she called to Hunter. She indicated the monitoring equipment on the ground. "I want to take that security camera back to the cabin."

"What are you planning, Erin?"

She paused. "We have nothing to warn us if someone's sneaking up on the cabin. I don't think it would take much for me to repair it."

"I like it. I'd feel a lot better if we had an advanced warning system. Keep using that sexy brain of yours, sweetheart."

His words fed a warm glow in her core. "With the quality of this equipment, I bet I could come up with a design that's tamper-proof." Erin could already see the circuits in her head.

They started back a different way. Hunter pointed out some of the local grasses and birds, and a short while later, they came upon a gurgling stream. With the Texas heat, it was a welcome sight.

"Want to stop for a while?" he asked. "I brought some food and something a little special in case we needed it."

Erin shifted in the saddle, and the baby started to fuss. "If I don't stop, I won't be able to walk when we get back to the cabin."

Hunter helped Erin down from her horse, then pulled his binoculars and some snacks out of his saddlebag. Brandon had been lulled asleep by the horse's cadence, but because of the jostling required for his mother to dismount, he was wide-awake now.

Hunter built a small fire, and Erin studied the water's ripple. "I didn't think west Texas had creeks."

"There's the occasional water source, but having this makes Logan's land all the more valuable."

Hunter looked around him. "This is the kind of place I've always wanted, you know. My mother and I lived in a tiny apartment. I slept on the sofa and I dreamed of wide-open space. That's one of the reasons I joined the military."

"My dream was a lot different than yours," Erin said softly. "I wanted to run a research lab and invent things that would make life better." She toyed with the grass brushing her legs. "I reached that goal, but it didn't turn out like I imagined. I guess after all this, I need a new goal."

Hunter lifted a package of marshmallows and chocolate. "How about we start with s'mores."

"You've got to be kidding."

"I got a hankering for them. We're in the middle of nowhere. Why not?"

She watched as he skewered the white fluffs on a stick and handed one to her. She let it toast and then suddenly the marshmallow erupted into a flame.

Quickly she doused fire with a few quick breaths. A crispy, crunchy, charred mess remained.

"Want a new one?"

Erin shook her head. "Hand me the chocolate and the graham cracker."

She trapped the marshmallow on the stick. The hard charcoal crust faded and oozed inner sweetness. She licked the sticky mess and looked up at Hunter.

"I finally figured you out," she said softly. "You're a burnt marshmallow."

"How do you figure?"

"You act all tough and hard."

"I'm a spy. Of course I'm tough," Hunter said.

She handed him Brandon and he kissed the boy's cheek.

"You're gooey on the inside."

Brandon rolled over on his back and grinned up at them. Erin blew a raspberry kiss on his tummy, and her son laughed. He reached out his arms to Hunter. "Da."

"He knows you're gooey, too," Erin said, a bittersweet realization that this might be the only time left for the baby to be with his father.

"I'll miss him," Hunter admitted. "I just didn't know how it would be. The reality of having a son is so much more than I expected. Leaving him…" Hunter paused and looked into Erin's eyes. "Leaving you both is going to kill me."

She took a deep breath. "What if you quit, Hunter? What if you got new identification along with us when we see that woman today? You could come, too. We'll find a place like this, far from all the conflict surrounding us. We could be a family."

Hunter didn't respond. He just stood with his back rigid and stared around him. The grasses swayed in the wind, and the creek gurgled, but he remained silent.

She couldn't believe she'd begged him. He loved Brandon. He wanted her, but she didn't know if he *loved* her. Oh, God, had she made a fool of herself?

"Forget I said anything—" she started, but he whirled to face her.

"I can't forget it."

She didn't expect the depth of the longing in his eyes.

He squatted in front of her. "Erin, look, I want to come with you. God knows I want every single thing you said, but I can't be sure my enemies won't find me. General Miller was right when he warned us that first day about the risk of having a family. I know now that I would do *any-thing* to protect you and Brandon." He stroked her cheek. "Even give you up."

Erin looked away, swiping at the tears building in her eyes. So she would be alone without him. Anyone else she would meet in the future would never know the real her. The Dr. Jamison who invented incredible crazy things. The shy, naive woman who'd been seduced and loved in a way she'd never known possible. They'd only know whatever made-up identity some unknown woman was coming up with today.

Erin Jamison would be gone. The only thing besides Brandon to go with her from this life would be her broken heart.

Hunter leaned into her. He kissed away the tears from her cheek. "If I could find a way, I would, Erin. I owe the general, but I would give up my life with the team with no regrets if I could have you and Brandon and keep you safe."

He shifted his mouth and took hers in a sweet and tender kiss.

If only he could find a way.

Her lips parted under his and she let out a low groan. He dragged her closer.

The snort of a horse burst them apart.

A large white animal crossed toward them, with Sheriff Redmond's little boy, Ethan, sitting in the saddle. He stopped and patted the horse's neck. "Are you two making babies? My new dad said all that hugging and kissing makes babies. I just don't get it."

Erin flushed, glad the kid hadn't come by a few minutes later or he might have witnessed that baby-making firsthand.

"Are you out here alone?" Hunter asked

"No, I just rode ahead on Sugar. He likes me, but you can't get too close. He's ornr...ornery. That means he doesn't like most people. He had a tough time when he was young, but he likes me a whole bunch."

Hunter stood and helped Erin to her feet, then settled Brandon back into his front harness carrier. "Who did you ride ahead of...your parents?"

"Yep, Dad's bringing Mom out in a car with lots of blankets. She can't ride horses 'cause of the baby." Ethan grinned. "It was all that kissing and hugging they did, for sure."

Chapter Ten

The narrow Texas county road leading to the woman who would make up Erin's and Brandon's new documents headed straight west. A few hills, lots of open spaces and no other vehicles as far as Hunter could see. He glanced at his watch. They were cutting it a bit too close to the scheduled meeting for his liking.

By the time he and Erin had delivered Ethan safely back to Blake and Amanda, the sun had risen high in the sky. They'd grabbed a quick bite for the road and changed Brandon, and now the SUV headed to a rendezvous point in the middle of nowhere.

The woman creating Erin and Brandon's documents was supposed to be out here. Somewhere. And she didn't wait for stragglers. Hers was a mobile operation and she didn't like staying in any one place too long. No exceptions.

Erin looked around dubiously. "Are you certain this is the right way?"

"According to Logan. A little farther and we should be there."

Hunter turned the SUV off-road, and the vehicle shot dirt into the air around them. The cloud of dust would be visible from quite a distance. He'd taken a few detours along the way, and hadn't seen a tail, but somehow the people who wanted Erin knew their location. He'd torn everything apart looking for a bug but had found nothing.

They needed to get the paperwork done and move on. Fast.

Finally, just over a small hill, he spotted a pickup truck with a nondescript tow camper behind it.

"Just like Logan described it," Hunter commented. "This woman must be paranoid as hell. There's nothing out here but mesquite and lizards."

He pulled up about twenty-five feet away from the camper, as instructed. Hunter removed his gun from the back of his pants and set it on the seat next to Erin.

"Move over to the driver's side. If something goes wrong, get out of here. Go to Blake and have him contact Logan. Understand?"

She gripped the weapon and scooted over as he exited the vehicle. "Don't let anything happen, Hunter. Please."

"No worries." He gave her a quick wink. "We'll be fine."

He trusted Logan, but Hunter couldn't ignore the tingling that had settled on the back of his neck. It had started the moment the team had attacked them at the Florida safe house. How had they known how to find them? The Zodiac assault on the *Precious Memories* had sent the feeling into overdrive. Now the warning signals hummed under his skin again.

"Halt. That's far enough," an electronic voice boomed through a sound system. "Who's with you?"

"Scorpion," Hunter said, providing her with the preagreed-upon code word.

"Stay where you are. I'll come out."

A small, attractive woman, her dark hair tied up in a topknot, emerged from the camper, an Uzi in her hand. "You Clay Griffin?"

So Logan had decided to use the alias. Good. One less person aware of his real identity. Hunter nodded and raised his hands in the air. "I'm unarmed."

She shook her head. "And I'm Little Orphan Annie. In fact, just call me Annie. Don't bother taking the knife out of your boot. I'm assuming you have a gun stashed somewhere, too."

Hunter didn't say a word.

"That's what I thought. Good thing Logan vouched for you. I don't like being lied to. Makes my trigger finger itchy." She stood fifteen feet away, legs apart, her stance aggressive and ready. She nodded toward Erin and Brandon. "Those the two I need to finalize the documentation for?"

"Yes."

"I didn't know one was a baby. I'll need two signatures for the passport—mother and father. You prepared for that?"

"Come up with a name, and I'll sign," Hunter said.

"Bring them inside."

She turned and rounded the camper to the door. He opened the SUV and faced Erin. "Let's do this."

Erin gave a slight shiver, but when she looked at Hunter, it was with confidence. He respected her for that. He grabbed Brandon's carrier and they walked around the trailer and mounted the steps.

When she entered, Erin gasped. Hunter didn't blame her. Half the place looked like a high-tech wizard's dream.

Annie stood in front of the camera. "Pictures first." She pointed to Erin, then at the stool. "Sit. And no smiling."

"I don't feel much like it anyway," Erin said, facing the lens.

"I hear you, sister." Annie snapped five photos.

Erin's countenance seemed sad and so very tired.

Hunter wanted to hide her and Brandon away at the top of a mountain somewhere and take all their troubles away, promise them everything would be fine. But he couldn't. A new life away from him was the only way he knew to protect them.

Annie stepped back from the camera. "Now the baby. Prop him up, but try to keep your hands out of the photo." Brandon jabbered and grinned at Annie, and she chuckled for the first time since they'd arrived. Her smile revealed a hidden beauty she'd taken pains to conceal.

She looked up at Hunter. "He's definitely your kid."

Erin grabbed Brandon and stood. "How can you tell?"

"The hair, the eyes and those dimples. Mr. Serious here doesn't smile that much, but when he watches you and thinks no one's looking he gets a goofy grin on his face. Those dimples show up then."

Heat flooded into Hunter's face. He couldn't believe he was so transparent.

Annie laughed. "Oh, don't sweat it, Clay. I make my living studying people and faces. Now sit down."

"You said you need my signature. You're not taking my picture."

"Sorry, but I need a fake identity for the kid's father. No choice."

Hunter paused for a moment, fighting his instinctive aversion to having his photo taken. The first rule of clandestine ops. No images. Whatsoever. It made you easier to find.

One glance at Erin and Brandon, though, and Hunter sat on the stool. As Annie said, there was no choice.

He would do anything for them, even if it turned out to cost him his life. Anytime. Anyplace.

Annie clicked the shutter. "I've chosen a name for you, Ransom Grainger. Like it?"

"Fine."

He couldn't take his gaze away from Erin. He wanted to soak in every curve, every line of her face. Each minute that passed ticked closer to the terrible moment when they'd have to say goodbye forever. That time was speeding at them much too fast for his aching heart, and not fast enough for their safety.

Annie nodded to Erin. "You're Marina Grainger, and your son is Brady. It's best if the new names are similar to your original ones. They're easier to remember. You're lucky your son is so young. He won't have any trouble adjusting." Annie looked at Erin. "You, however, will have the worst time of it. You're already fighting this happening. My advice? Don't think about what you *don't* have anymore. Think about what you *do* have. Not everyone is lucky enough to even get a choice."

A shadow crossed her face, then vanished as quickly as it had come. Annie jumped off her stool and strode to the table. She shoved several documents in front of each of them and provided two pens.

"Welcome to your new lives."

Hunter scanned the papers, signed and handed Erin the pen.

"Thanks, Hunter." Erin took the pen and bent over the documents.

"Don't forget to use your new names," Annie said quickly with a knowing glance at them. "It's the difference between life and death."

Erin's hand paused. "Oh, God, I called you Hunter—"

He covered Erin's hand with his. "It'll take time, but you can do this. All of it. I know you can."

Her gaze held his, but tears glistened. She nodded finally, biting her lip while she signed the papers. Hunter followed and stared down at their signatures.

Erin and Brandon Jamison were gone.

Ransom, Marina and Brady Grainger were born.

A family.

A family that never truly had a chance to exist.

Annie slid two more papers between them. "These are the last."

The divorce decree and custody agreement, granting Marina Grainger sole custodial rights.

The words ricocheted in Hunter's head. He glanced at Annie. "Are these necessary?"

"Marina needs full custody of Brady. You have to relinquish your rights as a father so she can make all the decisions for your son. There can't be any questions or any reason to search for Ransom Grainger. Ever."

Hunter clamped down on his jaw. His neck and shoulder muscles gnarled under the tension. God, the papers were fake; the situation was an elaborate lie, but the loss Hunter felt was devastatingly real. Annie's works had ripped his heart out.

After signing the first document, he gently chucked Brandon under his chin and stroked Erin's cheek. Her gaze lifted to Hunter's, pleading, and she gripped his arm.

When he'd kidnapped her a few days ago, no doubt she would've rejoiced if he'd signed over complete custody. He wouldn't have wanted to, but he still would have signed without hesitation.

Now he'd fallen in love with Erin all over again. She was different than he had imagined. Far more than he'd ever dreamed. She was smarter, braver, more passionate than any woman he'd ever known.

He could never tell her how he felt, though. He'd hold the truth inside him the rest of his life.

As to Brandon, that little boy had wrapped himself around Hunter's heart. He wanted to see what his son would grow into, what kind of man he would become. Brandon laughed like his mother. He grabbed on to life with both hands and with no fear.

Brandon was the best of both of them combined.

And Hunter would never see him grow up.

Hunter gripped the pen and signed his name to the custodial agreement. This was what he had to do. He had to give them up.

Ransom Grainger's signature made it official.

He was no longer a father. No longer part of a family that might have been.

A loud beeping noise coming from one of the panels on the wall echoed through the camper. Annie paled, rushed over and flicked on a switch. The streets of Carder, Texas, appeared on the screen. A large black car pulled up in front of the sheriff's office.

She let out a string of curses. "Let's finish up. I have to hit the road."

Hunter grabbed her arm.

She stilled and stared pointedly at his hand. "I don't think I'd do that, if I were you."

"Sorry," he said, releasing her. "Can I help?"

She shook her head. "My story, my life. You just live yours. You've got enough going on."

She finalized the documents, shoved them into an envelope and gave them the thick package. "Passports, birth certificates, driver's licenses from Montana. Along with the divorce and custody agreements, Marina and Brady should be able to start their new life without any trouble." Annie glanced at her watch. "Okay, that's a wrap."

She opened the trailer door. "We won't meet again, Ransom and Marina, but I wish you luck in staying ahead of whoever is after you. It's not always easy."

Hunter climbed down the trailer steps, then took Brandon from Erin.

Annie followed them out. By the time Hunter had secured Brandon in the backseat and shoved the SUV in Reverse, Annie had packed up her trailer and was in the large pickup heading into the middle of a field, no road in sight.

Erin leaned back in her seat. She looked over at Hunter. "I don't want to turn into Annie. She's all alone."

With a sigh, he gripped her hand. "You won't be. I know we've cut the ties to your old life, but I'll find you a new one that will be safe. You'll build new relationships. You and Brandon will be happy." He leaned over and kissed her lips.

"But it will be a life without you," Erin said.

"Yes," he said softly. "I'm so sorry, but it will be a life without me."

THE TEXAS LANDSCAPE ROARED past the SUV's window as Hunter sped back to the cabin. Once again he'd taken them on a tour of the back roads around Carder. At one point Erin wondered if they'd end up in San Angelo, or maybe even San Antonio. He'd gone in opposite directions for miles.

He was convinced they were being tracked somehow, and the knowledge had set him on edge. Erin couldn't imagine where the bug could be hidden. They'd all but stripped naked searching for the blasted thing.

Erin clutched the envelope with the documents for her new future in her hands. Her nails made indents in her palms. She wanted her former life back someday, but for now, she'd just take a day where she wasn't looking over her shoulder or didn't have to look at a dead body.

If that meant temporarily being Marina Grainger, she'd do it.

A week ago she would *never* have imagined saying those words.

As for Hunter, she sent him a sidelong glance. A week ago she'd never considered seeing him again. Now she didn't want to let him go.

And she had no choice.

Hunter pulled the SUV close up in front of the cabin. "Keep the gun handy. I'm going to confirm no one has been here before we take the baby out of the car."

He left the engine running and exited the vehicle, studied the door, then ran his fingers along the doorjamb and window frame.

His edginess had her jumpy, too. The thick envelope had gotten heavy in her hands. It contained all the documentation, plus a huge amount of cash Blake had given Hunter without a word, just a look.

Erin had been working with classified information most of her doctoral career, but nothing could have prepared her for the cloak-and-dagger life Hunter lived and breathed as if it were normal.

He had mentioned General Kent Miller several times, and how much he respected the man. Erin didn't know the depth of Kent's role in Hunter's life, but she did know that Hunter had changed and now he wanted out. There had to be some way around the no-family rules. General Miller might be the person who could make an exception happen.

Hunter motioned her with the all-clear signal he'd taught her. Erin clutched the paperwork and turned around Brandon. "Well, cutie, I guess this adventure is almost over. I'm trying to figure out a way to keep your daddy with us, but it's not looking good."

With a sad smile, she tickled Brandon's tummy and he laughed at her. God, to be so innocent again.

She followed Hunter into the house. They made dinner

and ate in silence, neither sure what to say to the other. Finally, she put Brandon down for the night, then moved to the kitchen table, where she'd plopped the broken surveillance equipment they'd collected on their ride.

"I don't suppose you have any small precision tools in that magical duffel?" she asked.

Hunter dug around the bag and pulled out a hard-sided yellow case.

"Your bag is as good as Mary Poppins's."

Hunter shrugged. "I'd feel better if it contained something that would identify their tracking device." He pulled out the tracker Leona had provided him and flipped it on. "No indication of any activity. I still don't know how they keep finding us."

"Then the least I can do is give us an early warning signal," Erin said. "Annie's system got me thinking. I need something that will warn us if someone is watching anywhere we are. It has to be portable and easy to use."

Hunter pulled up a chair and straddled it. "What have you got in mind?"

With a few quick twists of the screws, Erin took apart the camera and explained her idea. Hunter fired off question after question. He had an instinct for vulnerabilities in security that she'd never considered.

Together, they battled over the design, adding wiring and elements from a few of the lesser needed appliances in the cabin, until finally Erin sat back in her chair, satisfied. She flipped a switch, and the power light flickered on. The camera showed the interior of the cabin in high resolution. "What do you think?" She grinned at Hunter.

"Damn, Erin. You rock." He grabbed her to her feet and hugged her. "You're brilliant."

She closed her eyes, taking in that moment of his strong

arms holding her close, the warmth of his body pressed against her.

Love me, she begged silently. *One more time before I lose you forever.*

He stilled, as if he'd heard her plea, or he'd made one of his own. She held her breath.

Hunter cleared her throat and stepped back. "We should probably test it out. We'll be leaving in the morning, but tonight is still in the window of time that they've found us before."

Erin stared at him for a moment, disappointed.

She understood what Hunter was doing, staying vigilant for her protection, but that didn't make it hurt less. She should take Annie's advice. For the moment, she had Hunter in her life.

They would set up the warning system, as needed, but then she intended to make memories with him that would keep her warm for the lonely nights to come.

Erin opened the laptop and activated a wireless connection to feed the camera's data. She glanced up at him. She didn't want this to end. She squeezed his hand. She just couldn't give it a rest. No matter what Annie said. She gave it one last try. "We make a good team."

His eyes grew solemn. "Yeah, we do."

"Hunter, are you sure—"

"No, Erin. Don't ask again, please. I'll do anything for you and Brandon. Except put your lives in even more danger. If anything happened to you because of me, I'd never forgive myself."

HUNTER SCOOPED UP THE CAMERA. "I'll mount this outside now."

He had to get away from her, away from the severe constriction in his chest when he thought of Daniel and Noah coming to get her and the baby tomorrow. Hunter would never see them again. How the hell was he supposed to survive that kind of loss?

With a tug of the door, he stepped into the night. He turned once and looked back at Erin, standing there, the light billowing around her like a halo.

He'd never seen anyone so beautiful—or so sad. An expression he'd caused. Hunter prayed once this was over she would find happiness again. He doubted he would.

Slipping the small flashlight from his pocket, he flicked the red beam on to help his night vision, then closed the door behind him.

With a quick sweep, he visually scanned the area for anything out of place.

No movement.

The world was still, but that unease inside him told him to be wary.

He paused to listen. From the right, a lone coyote howled; an owl hooted, and a bevy of crickets chirped in the night. No unusual sounds, but the hilly area to the left seemed awfully quiet.

He drew his gun and stood silently analyzing the surroundings. Still not reassured, he figured he'd better get Erin's amazing camera up fast.

He glanced at the perimeter. The small mesquite a couple of dozen feet away from the house looked promising. The camera would be hidden. In the end, Hunter decided to go simple and secure it to the roof for the first test. He held the end of the flashlight in his mouth and reached for the low-hanging gutter. He attached the camera. If it worked as he expected, he'd scavenge Logan's ranch and Erin could build more. Since they were so portable, she could take them with her.

He couldn't be there for them, but at least the cameras

and alarm system would give Erin and Brandon a fighting chance if they were ever found.

A small click sounded far behind him.

Hunter whirled around, and a red beam flashed across his chest before settling into a familiar red dot.

Cursing, he dove to the side, but he wasn't fast enough. Something sharp jabbed into his thigh. Not a bullet, though. Hunter yanked the dart free, but it was already too late. His knees trembled, his arms went numb and he keeled over into the dirt.

Erin! His voice didn't respond. He tried to crawl to the door, but his muscles seemed frozen. A paralytic agent had rendered him immobile, but still aware.

In the silence, three black-clad figures ran across the front lawn.

Hunter panicked, desperate to move. Erin wouldn't know the men were coming. He hadn't had time to turn on the camera.

The attackers slammed open the cabin door.

"Hunter!" Erin's scream erupted into the night.

Please, Erin, grab the gun.

Hunter heard the sound of a fist hitting bone, and Erin went silent.

A gruff voice yelled, "Grab the kid. I'll take the woman."

No, Erin, no!

A large, dark SUV sped over the hill, spreading dirt and grit from its revving tires.

The men raced back outside with their prisoners, past where Hunter lay trapped in his chemical paralysis. He watched in horror as they tossed Erin's limp body into the back and handed off the baby. Seconds later, they were gone.

Erin! Oh, God, they'd taken her and the baby.

I'll find you, love. I promise. Stay alive, and I will find you.

THE DOOR TO LEONA'S OFFICE stood closed. Trace glanced at his watch. He'd had a meeting scheduled with her five minutes ago. He rapped his knuckles on the doorjamb again.

Still no answer.

This wasn't like her. Leona lived on Lombardi time—fifteen minutes early to everything.

He looked around but didn't see her rushing up to the door. Was she standing him up? She was angry with him, though he wasn't quite sure why.

To hell with this, he didn't have time. Too many strange things had been going down around here lately, and Trace didn't like it. He'd give her an additional two minutes; then he'd hunt her down.

Maybe she was in with the general. She'd been a bit secretive lately, and she and General Miller had started spending even more time together, often in closed sessions. That didn't bode well for the organization, or for the country. Those two had their fingers on the pulse of every terrorist organization in the world. They knew exactly when something big was brewing.

Maybe something broke and she'd been called away for an emergency meeting, forgetting about their appointment.

An uneasy feeling stirred in his gut.

For some reason, he didn't buy it. She hadn't forgotten. She never forgot. Anything.

He could live with the organization's secrets and the proverbial need-to-know situations that didn't always include him. That was part of the job, but something about the latest series of events involving Hunter Graham felt wrong.

The man had an exemplary career. Why go bad now? It didn't make sense.

Leona's door remained closed. Trace looked down the hall on either side, then tested the doorknob. It gave way and he walked in.

Empty.

That skitter of unease rippled through him again. A half-empty cup of coffee sat on her desk. A file remained open on her planner. That wasn't typical, either.

A tentative knock sounded behind him. "Sir? Is Mrs. Yates back yet?"

Trace turned. "No, Corporal. When was the last time you saw her?"

"She was headed downstairs to interrogate the prisoner."

Oh, hell. Mahew was insane. What if he'd broken loose?

Ignoring the corporal's shout, Trace raced down the hallway to the prison infirmary room. No guard stood outside the door. Trace swiped his badge and bolted inside.

The prisoner lay on the bed, staring with unseeing eyes, his hands still bound with restraints.

Trace let out a sharp curse. Had Leona killed him? Or had she stumbled upon a murder in progress? Cursing, Trace scanned the rest of the room.

Mahew's hospital tray lay on the floor. A chair had been tipped over.

Clearly a struggle had taken place, but between whom?

Several drops of red near the door caught Trace's attention. He bent down. He'd have the liquid tested, but he had no doubt it was blood.

Obviously not Mahew's.

Leona's? Someone else's?

Trace reached for the alarm, then hesitated. Too damn much was going on—all of it weird. A decorated hero like Hunter Graham suddenly tagged as a security risk. Leona Yates, Graham's handler and mentor, missing. A renowned nanorobotics engineer and her son made to appear dead, but alive according to the nonmatching dental records of the deceased, though that information had been destroyed—not buried, but destroyed.

Now Mahew was dead while in custody at the company. This, after being identified as a perpetrator in another explosion that had claimed at least one life and possibly involved Graham.

The long string of events had *insider* written all over them. But who was playing puppet master?

Trace tugged out his secure phone and dialed the general. No answer.

No way. First Leona. Now Miller. Trace contacted security to process the murder scene and strode down the hallway. Every move in this place was monitored. The security tapes would have the answer. He had to find Leona and Miller—and figure out who had killed Mahew.

Trace's gut told him Graham and Jamison were only a small piece of a very big puzzle. What the hell was going on?

If Hunter wasn't trying to sell the prototype to the highest bidder, then he was actually trying to protect the doctor and her son. Trace hoped Hunter would get the doctor and her child out of the cross fire soon…before it was too late. For all of them.

BRANDON'S SCREAMS PIERCED the night, and someone gunned an engine. Erin blinked and came to in the back of an unfamiliar vehicle. Her head throbbed. She touched the aching place on her cheek where the man had punched her. Pain seared through her and she realized it might be fractured. It was certainly swollen. Brandon cried again and she looked around,

Oh, God. Where was Hunter?

She peered out the back of the car to the cabin. Light streamed from inside the house, but she couldn't see Hunter anywhere.

Then Erin noticed a still body next to the cabin.

"Hunter!" He wasn't moving.

"He can't help you," the man bit out. "Keep your brat quiet or you're both dead."

Her mind went numb. Hunter couldn't be dead. Not after everything they'd been through, he couldn't be.

A masked man shoved Brandon across the backseat and dropped him into her arms. Her son was panicked and she held him close. He snuffled and burrowed into her.

Glass rolled up between the back of the SUV and the front two seats.

She banged on the partition. "Where are you taking us?"

"Sit down and shut up, Dr. Jamison. We have a ways to go."

Brandon lifted his head. "Mama...Da?" he said, his lashes wet with tears.

She closed her eyes and cuddled her son close.

"I don't know, little guy. I don't know if your daddy's okay or not."

Brandon patted tears coursing down her cheek.

She grabbed his hand and kissed it. "Mommy's hurt, baby. No touch."

Come on. You're supposed to be a genius. What would Hunter want her to do?

Thinking of him almost crippled her, but Brandon's life was hers to save now. Alone. She couldn't wuss out because she was terrified and heartbroken.

She peered toward the front of the vehicle. They were

headed down a dark highway. Only the dash lights shone in the car. In the back, where she was, it was nearly pitch-black.

Clutching Brandon tight, she used her other hand to feel for any kind of weapon, anything that would help her get out of this car. She'd heard the latch click on the lock, so she couldn't just open it and escape. She'd have to defend herself.

But with what? The back area was empty.

She ran her fingers over the carpet. Maybe there were tools or equipment stored underneath. If Hunter had done nothing else, he'd reminded her she could make something out of nothing. She would find a way to save her baby.

Erin shifted position to reach a new area of the carpeting, and near the edge, she came across a bump. She tugged the carpeting, and it lifted slightly. She moved out of the way and drew the flap of rug aside. Just beneath the floorboard she felt a metal handle. Was it the compartment for the spare tire? Her anticipation ramped into overdrive. She twisted the knob and felt a release.

A loud click echoed as the metal panel sprang free.

She stilled. Had they heard? She craned her neck. The four figures in the front of the vehicle didn't turn around, just kept arguing among themselves.

Carefully, she lifted the panel and explored the contents. After running her hand across the spare, she touched the tire iron. *Yes.* Gripping it tightly, she eased it out of the compartment and placed it beside her.

She had to be ready to defend herself and Brandon.

The moment the car stopped, these men would be in for a shock. She would not be passive and meek anymore. She'd make them pay for what they'd done.

To her son, to her and to Hunter.

She swallowed the emotions clogging her throat, and

rocked Brandon back and forth. She didn't even fight the tears flowing silently down her cheeks.

Oh, Hunter. What are we ever going to do without you?

Chapter Eleven

On the way to view the security camera tapes, Trace detoured into the facility's badge manager's office. "Do you have the information I called about?" he demanded of the woman behind the desk.

The manager looked up at Trace with concern. "You really want *Leona Yates's* records included? Do you realize the ramifications of your request when she hears about it?"

"I have my reasons, and I also have the authority to demand any person's records on this base. Isn't that correct?"

The woman stiffened. "Yes, sir."

"Then do your job and get the information for me. *Now.*"

Obviously troubled, she raced out of the office.

Tension clawed at Trace's neck and back like a beast tearing at flesh. Every move he made now could very well destroy the company...or his own career, if his suspicions were wrong.

He didn't think they were. He just hoped.

Within a minute, the woman thrust a stack of papers into his hand. "That's everyone's movements for the day. I hope you know what you're doing, sir."

Trace didn't answer. He just walked into the hallway, already searching the data for Leona Yates's identification and recorded movements. She'd come in, but she'd never left the facility. So where in the hell was she?

He checked her office again. Not there, and she didn't answer her phone or her page.

As he disconnected, the lab called.

"Padgett here. What did you find?"

"Initial tests show there's a ninety percent probability the blood from Mahew's room belongs to Leona Yates. I'll know more later."

Damn.

Trace put the phone in his pocket, his tension ratcheting up higher. The prisoner had been restrained so he couldn't fight back. Mahew wouldn't have drawn blood. So who did?

His stomach roiled.

He admired Leona. He had the entire time he'd worked for her. He didn't want to think she was involved in these events, but he'd discovered too many inconsistencies in her behavior, and the Caribbean bank accounts he'd just discovered had sealed the deal that something wasn't on the level.

Still, she was a brilliant operative. She wouldn't voluntarily leave her blood at a crime scene. He needed proof of her guilt—or innocence—fast.

He strode into the internal surveillance room and shut the door to the monitor-lined room. The private manning the booth looked at the closed door warily.

"Pull up the last three hours on camera fifteen," Trace snapped. "Play them on fast forward until I say stop."

"Yes, sir." The kid nearly passed out as he fumbled to follow orders.

Finally, the tech located the right view. The crisp images zipped by on the screen.

"Stop." Trace reeled at the images. Leona had gone into Terence Matthew's room, but she wasn't the creep's first visitor.

General Miller had entered first.

"Go back ten minutes and play it at normal speed," Trace croaked, unwilling to accept the truth that was about to play out. Again, Miller entered; then, several minutes later, Leona followed. "Keep the tape rolling in real time."

A short while later, Miller and Leona walked, huddled together, Miller chatting and laughing as if he were just visiting an old friend. Leona's smiles were more forced and she seemed a lot stiffer.

"Zoom in," Trace said. He squinted. He couldn't prove it, but given Leona's posture, he could swear that Miller had a gun to her side.

"Get out," Trace ordered the private. "I'll take over from here."

The kid squeaked an acknowledgment then hightailed it through the door. Trace's fingers flew across the controls, searching other hallways for another view of Miller and Leona. It was as if they'd vanished until…

Bingo. Miller escorted her into his office.

Ten minutes later, General Miller stalked out in full dress uniform. Without Leona.

What the hell was going on? Trace fast-forwarded through until the present. No one had entered or exited the general's room. Leona had to still be in there.

He raced to Miller's office and tried the doorknob. Locked. He keyed in his code and pressed inside, breaking more regulations than he could count. If the general court-martialed Trace, so be it. Once inside, he pulled out his firearm and walked into the room with its walnut desk.

Photos with Miller shaking the hands of the previous five presidents lined the wall.

Feeling as if he were stepping on sacred ground, Trace rounded Miller's desk and peered down at it. It was clean and pristine with the exception of a photo of his son in uniform that took up one corner.

The general had changed after his son's death. His work was more driven, the man less forgiving. That made his happy countenance on the video footage even more suspicious.

Trace, his gun at the ready, walked the room, threw open a closet door and scanned the interior. Only the general's private bathroom remained.

Where was Leona? Trace stared at the tiny bathroom, then stepped outside and looked again, mentally measuring the space. The dimensions were wrong.

Damn it, there was a hidden room. He tapped on the wall, knocking once, then again. "Leona?"

A barely discernible thud sounded from behind the barrier. Then three short taps. Three longer ones, three short again. Morse code for SOS.

Trace put his gun on the sink, ran his hands along the paneling and pressed against the wood. Finally, he felt a small indentation. He curled his fingers into the space and pulled.

A handle popped out, and he opened the door.

Crouched on the floor and covered with blood from a head wound, Leona blinked up at him, her face pale and sweating profusely.

"Trace," she gasped. "Thank God. We have to stop Miller. He's lost it. He killed Mahew."

Trace cupped Leona's elbow and helped her to her feet. She staggered and sat on the closed toilet lid. She pressed her hands to her head. "Oh, God. Miller tried to kill me, but he used too much drug on Mahew. For a moment, I thought I was dead. He never would have left me alive if he'd known my heart hadn't stopped."

"What happened?" Trace fingered her scalp, evaluating her injury.

She shook him off. "Let's just say he didn't much care what he tossed me against. Besides, my head doesn't matter. Miller got a call from the airfield that his plane was ready. We have to find out where he's going."

Trace pulled out his phone. "I'll call security."

She stopped him. "No. We don't know who's loyal to him. He got another call and said something about his men meeting him at the drop-off." She shuddered. "I can't believe this is happening. If you'd asked me two days ago, I would have killed for General Miller. No questions asked."

"Me, too," Trace said quietly. He helped Leona up. "Where do we start?"

"You search his computer. The monitor will have me seeing double and triple. I'll go through his private files," Leona said.

Trace hesitated. "You know we could be accused of treason."

Leona touched the still-bleeding wound on her forehead. "You're welcome to leave."

"Not happening. Whatever Miller's doing, he's misusing his office."

After helping Leona into the main room, Trace paused. "I thought he was a hero."

"He was," Leona said quietly. "It remains to be seen what he is now."

She stiffened her shoulders, walked around the desk and tugged open a drawer. With barely a hesitation, she flipped a switch. The back of the file slid down and another group of documents appeared.

Trace gaped at her.

"You learn a few things when you know a man for a

lifetime," she commented. "Can you drag me over a chair before I fall down?"

Trace settled Leona, then turned his attention to the general's computer while she searched through the files.

Trace pressed a few keys, but the system was locked.

He glanced at Leona. "Do you have the override code?"

Leona slowly nodded. They both knew that entering that code would set a chain of events into action that couldn't be stopped.

"Look away. I'll take the fall on this one." Concentrating hard on the keyboard, she typed in a long password.

The general's screen flickered on. Trace searched through a few documents on the desktop, then clicked a video file from the most recent files. It was the last thing viewed on General Miller's computer.

Grainy images blinked on the screen. The focus tilted, then jumped around a dark, dirty room with a steel bed and a stained mattress in one corner. On the dirt floor lay a young soldier in a torn uniform, bloody and beaten.

Leona stilled and stared at the screen. "Oh, my God. It's Matt."

"Matt Miller?" Trace asked. "The general's son?"

Trace turned up the volume and couldn't look away.

Curses and blows rained down on the defenseless man. Questions and taunts came from offscreen, but Trace recognized the voice of one man. Akbar Ali. One of the most brutal, sophisticated and dangerous militant leaders to hit the terrorist scene in years.

On the screen, a man backhanded the young soldier, screaming at him to beg for his life for the camera.

Matt Miller didn't beg. He kicked out his feet and took down two of the terrorists nearest to him.

Ali roared in anger, "Kill him."

One of the terrorists grabbed Matt's hair and pulled

it back, while another took a sword and cut off the soldier's head.

Ali laughed in the background. "Be warned, Americans. This is what we do to those who cross us. Don't expect mercy from me. Expect death."

The tape ended, but a moment later the grainy images started over.

Trace cursed. "The video is set to continuously loop. No wonder Miller has gone crazy."

"It's worse than that." Leona pulled out a file. "Miller has been in direct contact with Akbar Ali, using an alias as a weapons dealer. Have you heard of the op?"

"Ali is not part of Miller's current mission plans," Trace said. "I've been in every situational meeting on those operations, and Ali wasn't even mentioned."

Leona scanned the document. Her face paled. "Oh, Kent, what have you done?" She lifted a devastated gaze to Trace. "Miller is using Hunter and his family as bait. The general promised Ali that he'd hand over Dr. Jamison and her prototype."

Trace let out a long, slow breath. "Miller intends to be a hero one last time, and take down the terrorist who killed his son on American soil."

A LOUD COYOTE'S HOWL PIERCED the night. Hunter groaned, his head pounding and his movements sluggish. Dirt and gravel bit into his cheek. Confused and dazed, he pushed to his knees and stared around. Why was he outside? And what the hell was wrong with his brain and body? They weren't functioning right.

Disjointed images flashed in his mind. Men running. A red dot. The projectile in his leg paralyzing him. Curare, maybe? Ketamine?

He glanced at the open door to the cabin.

Oh, God. He remembered Erin's screams. They'd taken her and the baby.

His heart raced. He tried to stand. His limbs were still unresponsive to a degree, but he finally regained his balance and stood, swaying slightly. Through sheer force of will, he made it inside the house.

He grabbed a large flashlight and the keys, then staggered out to the SUV.

Slowly, he followed the tire marks to the paved road.

He'd lost them.

He grabbed his phone and punched in Blake's number.

"Redmond." The sheriff's voice was groggy with sleep.

"Erin and Brandon were kidnapped. I need whatever help you can give me. Without any public information. They're in a black SUV. Looks like they headed west on Old Market Road, but that's all I can tell."

"Do you have a license plate?"

"No. They hit me with some kind of drug. It incapacitated me. That's all I remember." He glanced at his watch. "They left here more than an hour ago."

"I'll see what I can do," Blake said. "But Hunter, if they didn't run a boatload of red lights or speed down the highway, they wouldn't have drawn attention. Call in whatever resources you've got at your end. You need more than a county sheriff's three-man office to find a missing black SUV in rural Texas."

Hunter paused. "Blake, these people are dangerous. They'll kill if they have to. Warn your people."

"Got it."

Hunter ended the call, then was struck by the realization that he was actually alive. Those guys hadn't killed him. So why just drug him? It didn't make sense.

He dialed Logan.

"Carmichael."

"It's Hunter. I need Daniel and Noah now. Brandon and Erin were kidnapped an hour ago, and I have no way to find them. Annie's got parts of Carder wired and can view them from her mobile unit. I need to know if she can tell me which direction a black SUV headed after leaving here. There were four guys."

Logan let out a string of curses. "If Erin and Brandon were taken an hour ago, they could be anywhere within five hundred square miles. We need to narrow the search."

Hunter scraped his fingers through his hair. "I've got to call Leona. Maybe she's seen something on satellite."

"That might not be such a good idea."

A cold chill encased Hunter's soul. "What are you saying?"

"We don't know where the leak is coming from or how they're tracking you, but Leona's one of the few people I know with the skills to set up something like this and get away with it."

With each word, Hunter's stomach knotted. More because he'd reluctantly come to the same conclusion. He didn't like hearing it aloud. He didn't even like thinking it.

"I'll get back to you with Annie's info," Logan said.

Daniel and Noah called and gave Hunter their updated ETA.

Desperate to uncover any clue to Erin and Brandon's whereabouts, Hunter searched the cabin once more. The men had taken nothing with them. Except his family.

His phone rang. Logan.

"What have you got?"

"Nothing. The SUV didn't go through Carder. They could be traveling off-road."

Hunter pounded his fist into the side of the cabin. "What the hell do I do now, Logan? How do I find them?"

LEONA TRIED TO QUELL THE throbbing in her head. She had to concentrate. Kent had gone over the edge.

She couldn't reconcile the man she'd fought evil beside for all these years with the madman who would sacrifice an innocent woman and child—and one of his best operatives—for revenge.

Heartbroken, she sighed. "I should have known Miller would want revenge. He handled his son's murder too well. Even though the general was devastated, he just completely immersed himself in work." She straightened. "We have to stop him before he gets to Hunter and his family, wherever they are."

"Leona, come here." Trace's voice sounded odd.

She peered at the computer. Trace was scrolling through hundreds of pictures of Erin Jamison and her little boy. An attached file showed locations, cell call logs, copies of day care interviews and even well-baby check notes from the clinic just outside Eglin.

"Miller's been watching Erin Jamison for a year," Trace said. He pointed to the name of a pediatrician. "This guy is on contract to us. I personally pushed through his security clearance last year at the general's request."

A shiver started at the base of Leona's spine and worked its way up. She scanned down farther. *Immunization. Brandon Jamison. TX9125. Insertion completed. Activated.*

Trace reeled back and met Leona's gaze.

"He inserted a chip in that baby? Oh, my God," she said. She pulled out her phone and punched in a number.

"You think Hunter will answer?" Trace asked. "I sure as hell wouldn't after everything that's gone down."

"He has to." Leona said a small prayer.

"Leona." Hunter's voice was reserved and suspicious on the other end of the phone.

"Listen to me. Please. Miller is behind everything.

You've got to get out of wherever you are now and keep moving. He put a tracking chip inside your son. You have to remove it or you don't stand a chance. That's how they keep finding you. They want Erin and the prototype."

"You're too late, Leona." Hunter's voice was flat, cold and dangerous. "They drugged me with a paralytic agent and took her. Brandon, too.

"My family is gone."

ERIN'S CHEEK THROBBED WITH A pulse of its own. It had to be broken based on the level of pain shooting through her face. She struggled to keep her mind clear, watching out the window, memorizing every turn, every road.

They'd just passed a giant roadrunner statue in Fort Stockton.

Now the men careened off onto a deserted road just outside the small Texas town, sending Erin tumbling. She kept hold of Brandon, but the tire iron slid, almost hitting the side panel of the SUV. She grabbed the metal bar before the sound gave away that she had the weapon.

The vehicle slowed and finally stopped. Her heart rate tripled. She could do this. She had to escape or leave a trail for Hunter to follow. She set Brandon on the carpet behind her, as far from the tailgate as possible, then turned to face the back of the vehicle.

She clutched the tire iron and waited, muscles taut with apprehension.

A flash of headlights reflected in the back window, somewhat blinding her. The four doors of the SUV opened, and the men stepped out to greet the newcomers.

Two rounded to the rear of the car. She'd hoped for only one. She'd have to move fast.

The tail lifted.

Erin didn't hesitate. She swung the tire iron like a bat and hit one of the masked men on the side of his head.

Bones crunched under the blow. He didn't even shout. He slumped to the ground.

Without hesitating, she swung at the other man, but he was too fast for her. He grabbed the tire iron and threw it to the ground, then yanked her forward and pulled back his fist.

"Stand down, soldier," a harsh voice ordered from the side. "I need her identifiable. She looks like she's already been beaten."

The attacker lowered his arm and backed away, glaring at her.

A man in full dress uniform walked into view. "Dr. Jamison. We meet at last. You're a bit more resourceful than I expected." He looked down at the crumpled man at his feet. "Maybe I should have recruited you for my team."

Erin took in all the medals across his chest and realization hit. "General Miller?"

The man Hunter trusted with his life. The man who she'd hoped would help her. He was behind all this?

Her body sagged.

"Duct-tape her hands and feet, then put her and the kid in the back of my car. And, gentlemen, make sure she can't reach any weapons this time."

They grabbed her and secured her hands behind her back before tossing her into the back of a white SUV, its engine still running. They thrust a squealing Brandon in next to her. He crawled over her body, crying to be held, but she couldn't. She could only nuzzle his cheek.

Miller slid into the driver's seat.

One of the black-clad men came up alongside and tapped the glass.

Miller slid down the window. "Yes?"

"Do you want us to follow you, sir?"

"No, I'll take it from here. Dump the SUV and return to headquarters. I'll debrief you when I return." He hesitated. "By the way, thank the men for me. You did your country a great service here tonight."

The man saluted.

Erin's gaze followed him and his two buddies. They picked up the unconscious fourth man and dumped him in the black SUV. Moments later, they hit the lights and started to drive away.

"You really have been a pain to deal with, Dr. Jamison. It's your fault I will lose four perfectly capable men."

He pressed a button, and the black SUV exploded into flames.

"Remember what you've seen. If that's the way I treat my friends, you don't want to be my enemy."

HUNTER HEARD LEONA'S GASP. She hadn't known.

Or else she was a damned good actress. He knew that about her already.

"Why should I believe you about Miller?" Hunter asked.

"Kent tried to kill me tonight, right after he murdered Terence Mahew. He's lost it. I should have seen it coming."

Hunter couldn't be sorry about Mahew, but he would never have imagined Miller would try to kill Leona.

"Graham, this is Trace Padgett. You have no reason to trust me, but we can help. Miller has taken the jet and he's heading to Texas. I'm assuming you're there."

Hunter remained silent.

"According to Miller's computer, the drug they probably shot you up with is a synthetic form of curare and nicotine. It was used in the fifties as a paralytic but abandoned because it was too dangerous. Miller's research teams worked the kinks out. If the info is correct, two hours after the injection, you'll regain full movement and your mental faculties will work as before."

"I don't care about myself. What's the frequency of the tracking device in Brandon? Can you find it?"

"Each chip is different," Padgett said. "I'm searching the database now."

Hunter groaned in anguish. "Hurry, damn it."

"Hunter," Leona said softly. "I'm so very, very sorry."

"Why did Miller take them?" Hunter asked.

"He's using them as a lure for Ali. The terrorist thinks he's getting Dr. Jamison and the prototype."

"Akbar Ali? The terrorist responsible for Matt's death?" Hunter cursed softly. He could understand the need for revenge. He'd seen Matt's decapitated body. If that had been Brandon…he'd kill the bastard.

But he would never use an innocent woman and a child to do it.

Not ever.

"Find them."

"I've got something," Padgett said. "When do Noah and Daniel get there?"

Hunter didn't answer. "I don't know what you're talking—"

"Scorpion," Padgett interjected quietly.

Hunter gripped the phone tighter. He recognized the code word. He also understood the leap of faith Padgett had just taken. And the connection he had revealed.

He'd been contacted by Logan Carmichael.

Trace Padgett was a man Hunter could trust.

Leona had remained still in the background, but Hunter could just imagine the wheels turning in her head.

"They'll be here in less than an hour," Hunter revealed. "Their plane has the equipment on board that can track the chip. Write this down." Padgett rattled off the frequency.

Hunter finished entering the numbers into his phone, and headed for his duffel. "If I get my family out of this alive, Padgett, we're going to talk. Then I'm buying you a drink. You, too, Leona."

"I think it will call for champagne," Leona added. "And formula."

HUNTER PACED AT THE END of the Triple C's runway, waiting for Noah and Daniel's plane to land. His body and mind were finally back to normal, if abject terror and fear counted among normal things.

Padgett had been right about the drug. Almost exactly two hours later, the effects had worn off.

Blake positioned his sheriff's car at one end of the runway, lights shining onto the pavement. Hunter waited at the other end to set fire to a line of lighter fluid. The airstrip was always used in the daytime, but both Blake and Hunter had seen enough drug plane setups to rig something similar here.

He glanced at his watch again, unable to believe only a minute had passed since he'd checked it last. Time was crawling, and Hunter was ready to lose it. Erin and Brandon had been gone for so long, and the grid pattern they'd have to search for one little tracking signal was getting bigger all the time.

Hunter's only hope was that Miller needed Erin alive.

Did he still need Brandon, now that Miller had the bait Ali wanted? Hunter prayed that was case. Even so, time was running out.

A plane's engine buzzed above him. The aircraft dipped one wing, then circled around. Hunter set the lighter to the fluid, and a line of fire rose into the air, delineating the airstrip.

The Lear landed with room to spare, not even close to mowing down the cop car.

Once the plane had stopped and turned around, Blake pulled his vehicle to the side. "I heard on the scanner that a black SUV was found burning near Fort Stockton a little while ago. I checked with local authorities there, and they just called back. They found evidence of explosives and four charred bodies inside."

Hunter's knees buckled, and he grasped the car.

"No. Hunter. None of them were a baby or a woman. I don't know if these were the same four guys who took Erin and Brandon, but someone is playing for keeps and leaving no witnesses. Be careful."

Hunter nodded but couldn't speak. The lump in his throat wouldn't let any words escape, even ones of thanks.

"Good luck, Hunter," Blake said. "If there's anything else I can do, let me know."

He watched the sheriff disappear into the night. Another man who'd proven himself worthy of trust, especially in a time of need. Logan knew some good people.

Would it all be enough?

The door of the Lear opened and Logan's partner, Daniel, peered into the night. "You ready to go, Graham?"

Hunter gathered everything up quickly and climbed into the plush plane. He filled in Noah and Daniel on the latest as he stowed his gear.

"Okay, the burning car gives us a direction to start. Buckle up," Noah said from the captain's seat. "I'm taking the fastest route south possible. We'll have a car waiting for us wherever we land. Soon as we see a signal, the order goes out."

Daniel limped over to the seat next to Hunter, instead

of going into the cockpit as usual. Hunter wondered how screwed up Daniel was after the torture he'd undergone in Bellevaux.

"You're not flying the plane tonight?" Hunter asked.

His friend shook his head. "Not my thing anymore. A little too tight quarters up there at night," he said, his grip white-knuckled. "Feels like I'm trapped in a closet."

"You okay to do this?"

"The shrinks think I'm nuts, but that's nothing new. I just happen to like wide-open spaces and big blue skies these days," he admitted.

Hunter studied Daniel, saw the scars on his face and hands. Would Daniel be all right? Hunter couldn't risk Erin and Brandon's safety if Daniel lost it.

As though he'd read Hunter's mind, Daniel lifted his gaze. "I won't let you down. I promise. Pissed off conquers fear, and this situation's done that and more for me."

Once they'd taken off, Daniel pulled out a metal briefcase from beneath his seat. He opened the case and flipped on a switch. "What's the frequency of your son's chip?"

Hunter pulled up the information on his phone and relayed the numbers.

Daniel recalibrated the receiver, and a tiny beep sounded. "We should be able to pick up the sound within a thousand-mile radius."

"They could have traveled farther than that."

Daniel sat back in his seat. "We'll grid the area out and find them." He laid out a map.

Hunter studied the southern half of the United States. "Their first pickup was scheduled on the Gulf of Mexico off the Florida coast," he said. "The burning SUV was south. If I wanted to make someone disappear, I'd get them out of the country as fast as I could."

"Miller has a plane," Daniel pointed out. "If he already picked them up…"

Hunter cursed. He refused to consider what might happen. They stared at the receiver, their tension growing with each mile of airspace eaten up.

Hunter knew Noah was pushing the Lear to its limit. It had been too long, and they still had nothing.

Suddenly, a buzz sounded.

Hunter studied the tracker, then the map.

"Got 'em," Daniel said, with a relieved smile on his face. "You were right, Hunter. They're not far from the border."

Hunter stared at the small moving dot. He touched the monitor as if it could connect him to his son and the love of his life.

He compared the two maps. "They're heading into Big Bend National Park. That's some rough terrain.

"Where can we land?" Hunter called to Noah.

"Lajitas," he answered. "They have a large enough airstrip. I'll have a car ready when we arrive."

Hunter bent down and checked his weapons and clips, then sheathed his knife. He met Daniel's gaze. "Top priority of this op is the safety of Erin and my son. No matter what else is going on. Agreed?"

Daniel gave him a solemn look. "We'll have your back, Hunter. We'll do what it takes."

"Good, because it's almost dawn and before this day is over, I'm going to take Miller down. Ali and anyone else involved in kidnapping my family are going to pay."

Hunter glanced at the dot, and his heart lurched. All movement had stopped. "You don't threaten what's mine and get away with it."

Chapter Twelve

Dawn broke over the mountains. The pink and orange rays of sunlight sliced through the mesquite and pine, highlighting the rocky crevices surrounding Erin like burning fire.

Miller had driven deep into Big Bend National Park, then gone off-road for several miles until they'd reached what he'd called their rendezvous point. "The nearby waterfall will mute a lot of stray sounds," he said with a smile. The way he said the words made her blood chill.

From the moment she'd witnesses General Miller's cold-blooded execution of his own men, she'd realized the man wouldn't leave witnesses behind. She had to find a way to get Brandon away from this monster. She had no idea what he would do next.

Now she sat at the edge of a small clearing, her hands still duct-taped behind her back. The baby was strapped in a harness that Miller had pulled from his vehicle. She was thankful. At least her son was near her.

Brandon was cold, wet, whimpering and desolate. She looked down to comfort him. Even that small movement set her cheek throbbing. Her face was swollen and her right eye barely opened anymore. She tried to keep the circulation going in her shoulders, but the angle they were tied at behind her back made them ache.

On the trip up here, she'd searched the back of the vehicle for at least an hour, hoping to find a sharp edge to cut the tape, but she'd failed. If Miller ever walked far enough away from her, she'd feel for a sharp stick or rock to use to shred the tape.

She had to find a way out, but she simply didn't know how to get away from this man. And no one knew she and her son were here.

She turned to watch Miller. With more light, maybe she could figure out what the general was doing. Knowledge was power, and she had to hold on to that hope.

Miller rounded the clearing, looking into the woods and listening, his weapon at the ready. He opened a small bag on his shoulder and rounded the clearing again, but this time he stopped every foot or so and stepped into the surrounding brush and trees. He'd crouch down, fiddle with something, then, a moment later, step back and move on to the next spot.

As he came closer to Erin, she studied him very carefully. When he stopped, he pulled a small device from the bag he carried and lined it up with the previous unit.

Oh, God, Miller was setting electronic versions of trip wires. Whoever broke the plane would explode a mine powerful enough to maim…or kill…anyone near it.

If the visitors triggered a mine on either side of where she and Brandon sat, they would be in the blast radius.

Miller glanced at his watch. "It won't be long now."

Erin shifted backward slightly so as not to attract Miller's attention, reaching her hands as far behind her as she could. She sifted through leaves, pine needles, twigs, but found nothing substantial.

Then her left hand brushed something hard. She paused and rubbed her thumb against the jagged edges of a stone.

Although elated, she forced her face to remain impassive. Erin grasped the small rock in her hands, grateful that it wasn't a smooth stone from the nearby streambed. No, this was hard and sharp and might just cut through the tape that bound her.

Gripping it awkwardly, she bent her wrists as far as they would go to spread the tape. Just a little nick, that's all she needed to get started. She rubbed the rock's sharpest edge against the thick tape, but it didn't give at all. She repeated the motion, over and over again, biting her lip in concentration until she realized Miller had looked her way again.

Erin schooled her expression into one closer to resignation and despair, which wasn't far from what she was feeling. She wished he'd turn away. She couldn't let him see that she was doing anything. But Miller needed to believe she'd given up.

She glanced down at her sleeping son. She was all that stood between him and death. And she would never, ever give up.

Miller tensed. He walked over to her and dragged her to her feet. Brandon nearly fell out of the chest harness and he screamed, glaring at their captor.

"Shut him up," Miller snapped.

"He's a baby. He's scared. Let my arms loose. He won't be quiet unless I hold him."

The screeching grew even louder. Finally, Miller cursed and sliced the tape between her wrists. "Keep him quiet or I swear I'll kill him. I'm too close to succeeding to have him blow it."

Erin jostled Brandon, trying to calm him and herself.

"Don't think for one moment you can get away from me," he said. "I've already proven *everyone* is expendable."

Pain splintered up and down Erin's arms as the circulation in her shoulders was restored. She gritted her teeth, praying Brandon wouldn't pick up on her distress and cry more.

She held him close, crooning nonsense words of comfort, and finally he settled against her chest and quieted.

A beep sounded from Miller's belt. He pressed her back against him and shoved the barrel of a gun against her ribs. "They're coming," he whispered in her ear. "Don't say a word. Follow my lead if you want to live."

Shock slammed through her. There was a chance? After killing his own men...

He shifted her to face south. A tall, thin man pushed through the bushes. Two men flanked him, their assault rifles pointed directly at her and Miller.

"Lower your weapons, Ali, or Dr. Jamison will be the first to die."

The man's eyes narrowed in anger, but he nodded at the men. They immediately turned their weapons to the ground. The three men stepped into the clearing. "You have made the entire transaction difficult from the very beginning, General. However, as you see, I can come and go into your country as I wish across this southern border. I am pleased to see you honored your part of the bargain. I don't like that my merchandise is damaged, however. Thankfully, Dr. Jamison's value is not in her beauty. Her skill will shine through her current disfigurement. Otherwise, you'd be dead already."

The man smiled at Erin, his snakelike eyes sending an icy quiver through her entire body.

Erin stood frozen. Miller was giving her to Akbar Ali? She recognized the psychotic despot from several briefings on terrorism. A ruthless and cunning man, he'd clawed and killed his way up the ranks of a once small-time militant group. The organization had been loosely run, with dozen of factions warring among themselves. Ali, after killing his competitors, had unified the disparate groups under one leadership that no one dared question.

Ali walked toward them. "I want the doctor now."

"That's close enough. I haven't seen any money yet."

Erin shot an incredulous gaze over her shoulder at Miller. Money? She was being sold to a terrorist for money?

Ali signaled and one of the men moved forward into the clearing. He knelt down and opened a small nondescript suitcase, then turned it around.

It was packed with U.S. dollars.

"Very good," Miller said. He took another step back.

Ali advanced. "Now for my prize," he said smoothly. "I have much need of her special expertise. You and I will cause quite a stir to those who doubt the…sincerity…of my intentions, Dr. Jamison."

Her stomach churned with disgust. Ali's eyes glowed with the promise of death. Hunter had been right. She never should have been so naive as to not see the weaponization potential of the prototype. The world could make anything good into evil. If good men let them.

Miller tightened his grip on Erin. "I have one more piece of business to finish with you." His hard voice carried a threat.

Ali smiled. "I doubt that very much, General. You would be a fool to take us on. You are one man. We are three. One shot to the head, and this meeting is over."

"Then you will never leave this clearing alive," Miller said. He pulled out a small remote device and pressed a button. "I've activated a net surrounding us. If anyone walks through, they will not survive."

"You're bluffing," Ali said.

"Try me."

Ali nodded to one of his bodyguards. "Go."

The man gave a slight bow and, without hesitation, walked to the edge of the clearing. He stepped forward.

One step. Two steps. Light flashed, and a loud explosion erupted. The man's body burst into flames, but he didn't scream.

He was already dead.

FROM BEHIND THE COVER of a large boulder, Hunter, Noah and Daniel peered through the cottonwoods and watched the plume of smoke billow into the sky. The acrid stench of burning flesh filled the air. Erin's terror and Brandon's cries shredded Hunter's heart.

"Go," Hunter whispered. "You know what to do."

Noah crawled on his belly, hidden by bushes until he reach the electronic trip wires. While the standoff in the clearing continued, he dismantled two of the mines with great care, then positioned himself behind Ali, ready to attack. Daniel did the same.

Hunter made his way around to where Miller and Erin stood, and dismantled another setup.

Ali and the bodyguard held their weapons on Miller, Erin and Brandon. "I don't see a winner for this game, General."

"It's not a game. You killed my son, Ali. You're dying today." Miller shoved Erin into the lone bodyguard. Erin dove to the side. The bodyguard raised his gun. Miller didn't flinch. He aimed his weapon and took out Ali with one clean shot to the temple, just as bullets from the bodyguard's gun strafed Miller's chest.

Ali fell back into a mine. Another explosion shot debris and body parts into the sky.

Hunter raced through the shrapnel and flames and tackled the surviving bodyguard to the ground. The man slammed his gun into Hunter's head and turned his weapon on Erin.

With one sharp move Hunter twisted the terrorist's neck.

The man lay still.

"Erin?" Hunter shouted, peering through the smoke

"Hunter!"

He saw her then, Brandon cradled in her arms. Behind her, Miller rose, the Kevlar of his bulletproof vest showing through his shredded clothing. He grabbed Erin when she tried to get up and pulled her to his chest.

"No," Hunter shouted. "Let them go. You got what you wanted. Ali is dead."

Miller gripped Erin close. "Damn it, Hunter. I didn't want you here. It wasn't supposed to go down this way. I don't leave witnesses. You know that."

"General, please don't." Hunter eased closer, his gaze on Daniel's and Noah's movements behind Miller. He had to keep the man's attention.

Hunter stared into Erin's eyes, trying desperately to convey that he had a plan, that he would save her. No matter what.

"What happened to you, General?" Hunter asked. "I thought I knew the man you were. You would never have sacrificed an innocent mother and child."

"You know nothing. Did you realize they were going to take away the organization I built from scratch? They said I was too old. That I should enjoy my golden years after all my exemplary service. No one was ever going to catch this bastard. He killed my son, beheaded him like an animal at the slaughter, and no one was going to do anything about it."

"Miller, I'm sorry—"

"Don't. Our company was fighting the good fight and those pansy-assed politicians were taking that away from me, too. Who would be left to make these murderers pay? They killed my son. They were going to destroy the company, and you…you were going to leave me, too. After all I did for you."

"What?"

"Matt didn't have to go back overseas on that last tour. He volunteered. Four times he went to that hellhole and came back alive. I wanted him to stay home and work for me, but then he met you. He admired you, Graham. Wanted to be like you. Save the world. So he returned and fell into Ali's hands, and *you* didn't save him."

Hunter felt the blood drain from his face. "Is that why you chose Erin?"

"Serendipity. The moment the information on her prototype came over my desk, I knew Ali would want it—and her. He came all the way to me."

Hunter stared at his mentor. "*You* were the leak? You told the terrorists about her prototype?"

"I needed to get Ali here. Kill him on my turf. I had it all planned out." He glared at Erin. "She screwed it up. With her and the baby gone, you wouldn't be distracted anymore. Ali would be dead. The team would get the credit. The politicians would reinstate the funds. Sure, there'd be collateral damage, but I'd explain away your name on those lists as part of our plan, and you'd stay on as my lead operative. Since I took out Exley, your stupid lawyer, your identity would be safe again. We would have done great things."

The general had truly lost his mind. "That's never gonna happen, Miller. This op is over."

Miller stared hard at Erin, then at Brandon. "I guess it is."

He aimed his weapon at Brandon.

"No!" Hunter grabbed the gun. They fought for control, knocking Erin and the baby to the dirt. She scooted backward toward one of the remaining booby traps at the clearing's edge.

"Erin, don't move," Hunter yelled.

Miller stared into Hunter's eyes and smiled, a sickly dead smile. *Oh, God.* Hunter glanced at Erin.

The general yanked hard against the gun, then with a sudden shift of weight forced Hunter off balance. He stumbled. In that instant, Miller rolled and lifted the weapon. "There'll be no witnesses!"

Hunter didn't hesitate. He leaped between Miller and his family, using his body to protect them. A spray of bullets slapped Hunter. He grunted and hit his knees.

Miller let out a deranged scream. He laughed at them. Hunter scooped Erin and Brandon and shoved them away from the clearing's edge. Miller couldn't stop his momentum. He tumbled into the trees.

The force of the explosion left nothing behind.

Hunter rolled onto his back, struggling for breath.

Erin crawled to him, crying. "Oh, my God, Hunter. Don't die. Please, don't die. I love you."

He let out a cough and shoved himself up onto his elbows. "Okay, I won't. You said the magic words."

Erin ran her fingers over his torso, shocked. "But he shot you."

"He's not the only one with a bulletproof vest, honey. Company rules for every op."

Erin burst into tears and he drew her close.

Brandon crawled into Hunter's lap.

"Da," he sniffled, exhausted and unhappy.

"Hey, sport." Hunter wiped the tears from his son's eyes, ignoring his own. "You've had yourself a rough day for a one-year-old."

Hunter hugged Brandon close, kissing his soft locks.

"If I lost you like Miller did his son, I'm not sure I would survive with my sanity intact, either," Hunter whispered.

"But you wouldn't risk innocent people for revenge," Erin said. She clung to Hunter's arm. "Is it over? Can I have my life back?"

Hunter looked over at Noah and Daniel. They wouldn't meet his gaze. They all knew.

"I'm sorry, Erin. Ali has been bragging about the prototype, and others want it, too. The chatter has gone wild. Your name's everywhere." He stroked his finger down her cheek. "You're the prototype's creator, and they want you. You'll have to stay dead or be hunted the rest of your life."

ERIN HELD BRANDON in her lap and listened to the roar of the cascading waterfall. The stream danced over the rocks and ended in a pool. If she'd had the energy, she would have washed the dirt and smoke from her skin, but nothing seemed to matter anymore.

If she was a normal woman, this would have been a beautiful place to camp, to lie under the stars or to make love beneath the cascading sheets of water.

Instead, Hunter, Noah and Daniel were still sifting through the scene. Hunter had ushered her out of the clearing as fast as he could, but he hadn't been able to hide the smoldering body of General Miller.

This would be a tough situation to explain, especially since she and Brandon were supposedly dead. No trace evidence of their being here could remain.

She kissed her son's head and laid her cheek against his soft hair. Everything inside her just wanted to shatter. Even breathing hurt.

Trees parted, the bushes shaking. Erin tensed, waiting as Hunter walked over to her. "Daniel and Noah will be set to go soon. They'll take you to Logan's plane and stop at various places to confuse where you're going. You'll be safe until you reach your new home."

"Where will that be?" She looked up at Hunter.

"I don't know. I asked them not to tell me," he said. He knelt beside the rock and cupped her uninjured cheek. "If I knew where you were, I don't know if I could stay away from you."

Erin wanted nothing more than to lean into his touch. "But you're sending us away anyway. Ali is dead. Miller is dead."

"With my ties to Miller and my past ops, I'm on more assassination lists than I can name. I won't risk you or our son."

She clutched at his shirt. "Find a way to be with me. I know you can."

"If I do—" he kissed her nose "—I'll find you. Somehow, I will. I promise, Erin."

Daniel and Noah pushed their way through the trees. "It's time."

Erin's eyes filled. "I love you, Hunter. I always will."

He pressed a gentle kiss to her forehead, but didn't say the words back to her. He'd never actually said the words.

The realization made her entire body freeze.

She held Brandon close and stood. "I understand," she lied. "I was fine before. I'll be fine again. Just me and my son. The way it's always been."

Hunter simply stared, the anguish in his eyes devastating. But he remained silent.

Her heart breaking, Erin followed Noah and Daniel back to an SUV standing in wait. They loaded what little she had collected with Hunter over the past few days into the back.

Hunter opened the door and placed Brandon in the car

seat. He rested his lips on his son's hair. "Goodbye," he whispered.

She slid into the backseat and rolled up the window. She couldn't stop the tears flowing down her cheeks as the car pulled away. She didn't look back, just whispered one last time, "Goodbye, my love. You will always have my heart."

"RANSOM!" LEONA'S VOICE called out from the next room at Logan's ranch.

Hunter was securing some equipment in the bunker, and he bumped his head trying to get out from beneath the desk.

"Ransom!" she called again.

"Give me a minute, Leona," Hunter groused. He still didn't know when he'd get used to his new name, but it broke his heart every time he heard it. He'd thought of changing it again, but it was the last bond he had with Erin and his son. Fictitious names for a fictitious family. In his heart, it was all real.

Leona had worked her magic. Even the company believed he was dead. "Hunter Graham" had been killed in an automobile accident in New Orleans not far from his home. "Clay Griffin" had met his Maker in a small plane crash over the Mediterranean. Now only Ransom Grainger existed. A broken man with a shattered past. He wondered if he'd ever be okay again.

He wiped his face with a rag and crawled out from beneath the console.

Logan had called and as of two weeks ago, Clay's name had been scrubbed from the assassin watch lists. Ali's terrorist organization had taken credit for the hit. One last act in honor of their fallen leader.

Trace Padgett had let him know that the terrorist group had scattered. At least for now.

Hunter had been fantasizing about finding Erin. Maybe, if things continued the way they were, he could finally do that in a year or so.

If he was lucky, it might not be too late.

Frustrated, Hunter straightened and surveyed Logan's underground bunker. It looked better now. It had taken a month of dirty, intensive work to clean up, but the generator had been repaired, the new electronics installed and Hunter had just put up the last of Erin's camera design at the front gate for testing.

Damn it, he missed her. He missed her brainy observations, her beautiful smile, her love for their son.

If Erin's loss had shattered Hunter's heart, Brandon's loss had eviscerated him. He wanted to teach his little boy to ride and rope and have fun on a ranch. He wanted to teach him to have solid convictions and stand by them. He wanted to have that talk with him about girls.

None of it would happen.

Was there any worse feeling than what might have been?

"Ransom. You have a phone call. It's Logan." Leona looked down at him from the escape hatch and tossed him the secure satellite phone.

"What's up, Your Highness?" Hunter smiled for the first time in days.

"Stow it, *Ransom*," Logan countered. "Are you used to it yet?"

"It'll come."

"I may never get used to your new name, but I'll try."

Hunter sat back in a folding chair and stared at the open hatch. The July sun beat down on him through the opening. "What's going on? I know we're spending a lot of money—"

"That's not the issue." Logan took a deep breath. "Kat and I have been talking. While we'd like to visit the ranch to get the kids away from this crazy palace life, I won't have the time to commit to the company. Not like we discussed." He lowered his voice. "Kat's pregnant, and I need to be here for her. She needs me to take on more responsibilities in Bellevaux. I have to bow out, Hunter."

Hunter's stomach dropped. "I understand. Family is the most important thing, Logan. I learned that the hard way. Do you want me to stop work?"

"No way. Covert Technology Confidential, Incorporated, is needed. Just not with me at the helm. People like Annie need us. I want you to run CTC, Hunter."

Hunter fell back in his chair and hit his head on the concrete floor. He blinked. "You can't be serious. What about Daniel?"

"He's AWOL at the moment. He needs time. When he's ready we'll bring him back in, if he wants to be part of CTC." Logan paused. "You've been ready for this a long time, Hunter. With Leona and Chuck to help you, I don't see how you won't succeed."

Hunter picked himself off the floor and paced back and forth, his mind whirling with ideas. CTC would be a way to give back, to help those who couldn't help themselves. The organization would give people like Annie and Erin a chance at a life when there seemed to be nowhere to turn. And his life would have purpose again. Even if his heart was broken. "You've got yourself a deal," he agreed. "Partner."

He ended the call, stunned, and looked around the room. Empty. No one here with whom to share his new life. What he wouldn't give to have Erin next to him.

An alarm sounded at the console he'd just hooked up. The front gate. He activated the camera.

A black SUV sat parked in front of the newly erected

barrier. Hunter tensed, his hand reaching for a weapon. He wasn't expecting anyone.

The door opened and a dark-haired woman with long, slim legs stepped into the sun.

She looked into the camera and smiled.

She was beautiful, and his stomach gave a jolt. There was something familiar...

She reached into the backseat and pulled out a baby carrier. She lifted a small boy into her arms, pointed up to the camera and waved.

The baby let out a big grin.

Hunter swayed.

Brandon.

He vaulted out of the exit and sprinted to the gate. When he reached the edge of the property, he skidded to a halt.

A stranger stood before him. But not a stranger.

He studied her features, then stared into her eyes. Emerald-green, with a smile hidden behind them. Maybe not so innocent anymore, but honest and forthright.

He knew those eyes, only her face and hair color were different.

"Erin...."

She tilted her head. "So, what do you think of my new look? The color is still in the experimental stage, but this one's not bad."

Hunter swallowed, unable to believe she was standing there.

He pressed the release button, and the gate swung open. He stepped through. His shaking hand hovered over her high cheekbones, traveled across her narrowed nose and down to her fuller lips. "What did you do?"

She bit her lip, that nervous habit that made him want to hold her and make everything better.

"My cheekbone was shattered. They had to do reconstructive surgery, so I decided if I couldn't be Erin Jamison anymore, the least I could do was start over completely. I don't want to look over my shoulder all the time. And, I hoped, if no one could recognize me, maybe…maybe I could have what I really want."

He held his breath, afraid to hope.

"More than any career as a scientist, more than fame or accolades, I want you, Hunter. I think you love me. I hope I'm not wrong."

His chest tightened. He drank in her presence. She was everything he ever wanted. She made his life complete. "I love you more than life itself. You and Brandon."

The words tumbled out of him, words he'd longed to say for nearly two years.

She threw herself into Hunter's arms.

Noah exited the SUV and dropped two suitcases at Hunter's feet. "Don't screw this up, *Ransom*. I wish I could find a woman who loves me like she does you."

His friend jumped into the SUV and took off toward the highway leading away from the CTC Ranch.

She looked over Hunter's shoulder. "I see you installed my camera design."

He smiled. "It's brilliant. Why wouldn't I use it?"

She clutched his shirt, her expression earnest. "Let me be a part of this. Noah told me about CTC. I can help. Let me use my talents to save people. Let me be what I was meant to be. Here, with you. As Marina Grainger. We make a great team."

Was he dreaming? "Are you sure?"

Erin gripped his fingers. "This is my choice, Clay, Hunter, Ransom…or whoever you are today. I love you. I go to sleep dreaming of you. My heart misses you. My mind misses you. No one else makes me feel the way you do. I watched you fight to save our lives. Now I'm fight-

ing for your heart. You're my son's father, and I won't let
you go. Not again."

She held his face in her hands. "Do you truly love me?"

Hunter couldn't stop the indescribable joy welling inside of him. His heart burst from within. He wouldn't let
his dream slip through his fingers, not again.

"I fell in love with you the moment I saw you on that
beach in Santorini and you started lecturing me about that
shell. You were so alive. So excited. I'd never known what
hope was until I found you. I love you, Erin."

"Marina," she whispered, wrapping her arms around
him. "No matter what our names, our hearts will always
know each other."

"Da!" Brandon called out.

"Good thing that name still works." Hunter released
Erin, and looked down at his son. He picked him up and
cuddled the boy.

"Da...da...da."

With a sigh, he pulled Erin close into his arms. "I'll do
everything in my power to protect you both. I promise."

She laid her head against his shoulder. "No. This time,
my love, we'll protect each other."

He tugged her dark hair. "It's the same color as Brandon's now. Do I need a disguise? Do you think I'd look
good as a blond? Or I could shave my head?"

"Or, Mr. Grainger—" she kissed Hunter "—you could
take me up to the cabin and make love to me all night
long."

He could feel the passion and the love through every
caress of her lips. Hunter held her close, relishing the feel
of her body against his. These curves, he remembered. He
spun her around. "I like your ideas so much better than
mine, Marina. You are a genius. Now

    let's go be a family."

Her eyes shining, she gazed up at him. "Does this mean we have to get remarried, Mr. Grainger?"

Her tear-filled eyes held such hope and such love, he couldn't breathe. He hugged his family close and closed his eyes, sending a prayer to heaven. He would never let them go.

"It most assuredly does, Mrs. Grainger. And I know the perfect beach in Santorini for a honeymoon."

* * * * *

COMING NEXT MONTH from Harlequin® Intrigue®
AVAILABLE JUNE 18, 2013

#1431 OUTLAW LAWMAN
The Marshals of Maverick County
Delores Fossen

A search for a killer brings Marshal Harlan McKinney and investigative journalist Caitlyn Barnes face-to-face not only with their painful pasts but with a steamy attraction that just won't die. Only together can they defeat the murderer who lures them back to a Texas ranch for a midnight showdown.

#1432 THE SMOKY MOUNTAIN MIST
Bitterwood P.D.
Paula Graves

Who is trying to make heiress Rachel Davenport think she's going crazy? And why? Former bad boy Seth Hammond will put his life—and his heart—on the line to find out.

#1433 TRIGGERED
Covert Cowboys, Inc.
Elle James

When ex-cop Ben Harding is hired to protect a woman and her child, he must learn to trust in himself and his abilities to defend truth and justice...and allow himself to love again.

#1434 FEARLESS
Corcoran Team
HelenKay Dimon

Undercover operative Davis Weeks lost everything when he picked work over his personal life. But now he gets a second chance when Lara Barton, the woman he's always loved, turns to him for help.

#1435 CARRIE'S PROTECTOR
Rebecca York

Carrie Mitchell is terrified to find herself in the middle of a terrorist plot...and in the arms of her tough-guy bodyguard, Wyatt Hawk.

#1436 FOR THE BABY'S SAKE
Beverly Long

Detective Sawyer Montgomery needs testimony from Liz Mayfield's pregnant teenage client, who is unexpectedly missing. Can Sawyer and Liz find the teen in time to save her and her baby?

You can find more information on upcoming Harlequin® titles, free excerpts and more at www.Harlequin.com.

HICNM0613

REQUEST YOUR FREE BOOKS!
2 FREE NOVELS PLUS 2 FREE GIFTS!

✦ HARLEQUIN®

INTRIGUE®

BREATHTAKING ROMANTIC SUSPENSE

YES! Please send me 2 FREE Harlequin Intrigue® novels and my 2 FREE gifts (gifts are worth about $10). After receiving them, if I don't wish to receive any more books, I can return the shipping statement marked "cancel." If I don't cancel, I will receive 6 brand-new novels every month and be billed just $4.74 per book in the U.S. or $5.24 per book in Canada. That's a savings of at least 14% off the cover price! It's quite a bargain! Shipping and handling is just 50¢ per book in the U.S. and 75¢ per book in Canada.* I understand that accepting the 2 free books and gifts places me under no obligation to buy anything. I can always return a shipment and cancel at any time. Even if I never buy another book, the two free books and gifts are mine to keep forever.

182/382 HDN F42N

Name _____ (PLEASE PRINT) _____

Address _____ Apt. # _____

City _____ State/Prov. _____ Zip/Postal Code _____

Signature (if under 18, a parent or guardian must sign)

Mail to the **Harlequin® Reader Service:**
IN U.S.A.: P.O. Box 1867, Buffalo, NY 14240-1867
IN CANADA: P.O. Box 609, Fort Erie, Ontario L2A 5X3
**Are you a subscriber to Harlequin Intrigue books
and want to receive the larger-print edition?
Call 1-800-873-8635 or visit www.ReaderService.com.**

* Terms and prices subject to change without notice. Prices do not include applicable taxes. Sales tax applicable in N.Y. Canadian residents will be charged applicable taxes. Offer not valid in Quebec. This offer is limited to one order per household. Not valid for current subscribers to Harlequin Intrigue books. All orders subject to credit approval. Credit or debit balances in a customer's account(s) may be offset by any other outstanding balance owed by or to the customer. Please allow 4 to 6 weeks for delivery. Offer available while quantities last.

Your Privacy—The Harlequin® Reader Service is committed to protecting your privacy. Our Privacy Policy is available online at www.ReaderService.com or upon request from the Harlequin Reader Service.

We make a portion of our mailing list available to reputable third parties that offer products we believe may interest you. If you prefer that we not exchange your name with third parties, or if you wish to clarify or modify your communication preferences, please visit us at www.ReaderService.com/consumerschoice or write to us at Harlequin Reader Service Preference Service, P.O. Box 9062, Buffalo, NY 14269. Include your complete name and address.

HI13R

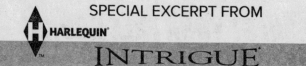
*When mysterious threats are made on the lives of
Kate Langsdon and her young daughter, only decorated
former Austin police officer Ben Harding is willing to
protect them at any cost.*

The warmth of his hands on her arms sent shivers throughout her body. "Really, it's fine," she said, even as she let him maneuver her to sit on the arm of the couch.

Ben squatted, pulled the tennis shoe off her foot and removed her sock. "I had training as a first responder on the Austin police force. Let me be the judge."

Kate held her breath as he lifted her foot and turned it to inspect the ankle, his fingers grazing over her skin.

"See? Just bumped it. It'll be fine in a minute." She cursed inwardly at her breathlessness. A man's hands on her ankle shouldn't send her into a tailspin. Ben Harding was a trained professional—touching a woman's ankle meant nothing other than a concern for health and safety. Nothing more.

Then why was she breathing like a teenager on her first date? Kate bent to slide her foot back into her shoe, biting hard on her lip to keep from crying out at the pain. When she turned toward him she could feel the warmth of his breath fan across her cheek.

"You should put a little ice on that," he said, his tone as smooth as warm syrup.

Ice was exactly what she needed. To chill her natural reaction to a handsome man, paid to help and protect her, not touch, hold or kiss her.

Kate jumped up and moved away from Ben and his gentle fingers. "I should get back outside. No telling what Lily is up to."

Ben caught her arm as she passed him. "You felt it, too, didn't you?"

Kate fought the urge to lean into him and sniff the musky scent of male. Four years was a long time to go without a man. "I don't know what you're talking about."

Ben held her arm a moment longer, then let go. "You're right. We should check on Lily."

Kate hurried for the door. Just as she crossed the threshold into the south Texas sunshine, a frightened scream made her racing heart stop.

Don't miss the dramatic conclusion to
TRIGGERED by Elle James.

Available July 2013, only from Harlequin Intrigue.